BLUE FINGERS

A Ninja's Tale

by Cheryl Aylward Whitesel

Clarion Books ■ New York

To Paul,
my very own *jonin*

And to Ross,
born with the heart of a *ninja*

*I would like to thank Hatsuko Romero for reading this
manuscript and advising me about the rich and beautiful
culture of her native Japan.*

Clarion Books
a Houghton Mifflin Company imprint
215 Park Avenue South, New York, NY 10003
Copyright © 2004 by Cheryl Eileen Whitesel

The type was set in 12-point Bembo.

www.houghtonmifflinbooks.com

Printed in the U.S.A.

Library of Congress Cataloging-in-Publication Data
Whitesel, Cheryl Aylward.
Blue fingers : a ninja's tale / by Cheryl Whitesel.
p. cm.
Summary: Having failed apprenticeship as a dye maker, Koji is captured
and forced to train as a ninja, where he remains disloyal until he
discovers samurai have burned his former village.
ISBN 0-618-38139-2
1. Japan—History—Period of civil wars, 1480–1603—Juvenile fiction.
[1. Japan—History—Period of civil wars, 1480–1603—Fiction.
2. Ninja—Fiction. 3. Samurai—Fiction.] I. Title.
PZ7.W58785 Bl 2004
[Fic]—dc22   2003016870

MV   10   9   8   7   6   5   4   3   2   1

Iga Mountains, Japan
1545

Koji peeked between the rain shutters of the thatched farmhouse and watched for his twin brother. The rain was pelting down hard. "I can't make out the path," he said over his shoulder.

Papa spoke. "Kojiro. Keep watching."

Koji frowned. He didn't like Papa to call him by his full name. It meant he'd better behave.

As Koji turned back to the window, Taro burst in from outside. He flung off the torn piece of straw mat he'd held over his head to keep off the rain. He scattered water like a shaking dog. His basket rolled into one corner, and a live eel slid out along the fallen walking stick he had carved himself.

"You'll never believe it!" Taro said, gasping as he dived for the eel. His aim was perfect, and he whipped it back into the basket. "I went to the fish peddler. I stayed way up on the riverbank like you said, Mama. But the water was wild and—"

"If I'd known it was dangerous . . . ," Mama murmured.

Papa swung around to face Taro's twin. "Kojiro, if you'd gone with your brother, you would have protected each other."

"I was just slow. I didn't mean to—"

"What use is 'didn't mean to'?" Papa scolded. "Taro's always there for you, while you, the elder—"

"Don't blame him, Papa. You know how he can be sometimes." Taro gave Koji's shoulder a fond push. "So I heard a shout . . ."

Taro's description of his errand to the fish shop on the riverbank had barely tumbled out of his mouth when there was a knock. Whoever stood thumping on the door frame must be using his fist to be heard over the torrent. Papa started for the door.

The twins slipped through the *shoji* screen, the sliding, wood-framed paper partition, into the other room. "You're a hero, Taro," Koji whispered, concentrating on keeping his smile wide. But he couldn't stop a pang from shooting through his heart. *Why couldn't I have been there with Taro?* he wondered. *Then Mama and Papa would look proudly at me.*

"Koji, look," Taro whispered. The boys peeked into the main room, where the hearth fire cast a soft glow. Silhouetted in the open doorway, a big man was slipping out of his high wooden sandals, or *geta,* to come inside. He dropped an oiled paper umbrella beside his shoes under the deep eaves, where the ground was dry. Never had anyone in such a glossy black *kimono* set foot in this house. The kimono was dripping wet, and so was the man's hair.

The twins huddled together, Taro with one hand against Koji's chest as if to hold him back in case he went blundering into the main room. On the other side of the paper wall, the shapes of their parents were silhouettes in front of the flickering candle flame. They kept bowing and bowing to the stranger.

"I am Tanaka Shinzaemon, master dye maker to Lord Udo. I came to talk to you about your brave son. He saved my life." The man went on in a low rumble, barely audible to the boys over the roaring rain. They peered through the slits between the moonlit shutter slats as they strained to hear.

"I slipped and was swept into the river," the big man went on. "Your boy snatched up the pole that always leans against the fish shop—the one old Ryoshi slings across his shoulders to carry baskets of fish. Your son used it to pull me out of the water, but once I was safe, he ran off. I followed to thank him."

"He'll reward you, Taro," Koji whispered. "Rice. Even money!"

Taro clamped his teeth shut on his lower lip as if to stop himself from shrieking with excitement. Then he gripped Koji by both shoulders. "Whatever it is, we'll share down the middle."

"Oh, Taro," Koji murmured, looking down shyly.

In the other room, their stunned parents were silent.

"Where is your boy? And how old is he?"

"Why, twelve."

"Good, that's old enough. He's clever. Nimble, too. Perfect! Then I have a proposition for you. I need an apprentice at my dye shop, the *someru-ya*. If you'll let him accept, I need to take him away now because—"

Take him away! I wouldn't go away with that big man if I were Taro, Koji thought. He turned to his brother. "I can't take half of your reward," he said with relief. "But I don't want you to go, either. I—"

"Shh!" Taro commanded.

The twins heard more conversation, and then their father appeared before them.

"Is he serious, Papa?" Taro asked, flushed and wet. "Would such an important man really give me a chance in life?"

"So he says. Unbelievable, and I'm so proud of you!"

But Mama appeared behind Papa. "Wait," she whispered. "Should we send Taro? Or . . ." Her glance went to Koji. "Don't forget about . . . We should have told the boys long ago."

Papa glanced over his shoulder at her, and a meaningful look passed between them.

"You're right," Papa murmured. "It can wait no longer." He turned to the twins. "Boys, when you were born—"

From the other room their guest called, "I'm sopping wet. Please decide."

"We don't have time to explain to the twins now,"

Papa whispered to Mama. "But you're right. Koji must be the one to go. He'll be right there, Tanaka-*sama*," he called.

Mama touched Koji's cheek, then Taro's. "We love you."

Papa pulled Koji to his feet and stared into his eyes. "Koji, follow your destiny."

"But Papa—" Taro began.

"Destiny?" Koji said. "I don't understand."

"You don't need to understand. Not now. Just hear." Papa went to the porcelain water jar and removed its wooden lid.

"Papa?" Taro prompted again.

Papa laid his hand on Taro's shoulder, but he spoke to Koji. "Wet your head, Kojiro, as if you've been out in the rain. *You* have to go with Tanaka-sama."

"I won't! I don't want to leave you and Mama, and I won't be separated from my twin brother."

"Hush!" Papa glanced around at the shadow of the master dye maker on the paper wall. "You know how unlucky most people think twins are. Never mention that word in front of Tanaka-sama." Papa pushed Koji's head under the water as Taro gaped enviously.

Koji came up gulping. Water streamed from his hair. "Why me?" he sputtered. "It's not my fault I'm a moment older."

"That has nothing to do with our decision. But when you were born—" Mama began.

"Is he coming?" the master dye maker called again.

"Remember, you were the one at the fish shop,

Koji," Papa said urgently. "You saved Tanaka-sama's life."

Mama pressed into Koji's hand a little wooden statue of Jizo, the patron of children. Papa had carved it when the twins were younger. Koji and Taro had prayed to it countless times. "Jizo-sama will keep you safe." She closed his fingers around it. "Hold him near and know we are with you."

Koji pushed the Jizo at his mother. "Don't make me go."

But Papa clapped a hand over Koji's mouth. "He's coming!" he called to the master dye maker. "He's changing into dry clothes!" He snatched the Jizo and tucked it under the overlapping lapels of Koji's *haori*. "Remember: say nothing about being a twin. And Taro, stay in this room until they're gone."

"Here he is, Tanaka-sama," Papa said a moment later, bowing as he nudged Koji toward the big stranger. "My lowly son is unworthy of the fine position you offer," he added, beaming.

With a broad smile across his stern face, the master dye maker looked Koji up and down. "He is worthy. I've seen what stuff he's made of. If not for you," he added, leaning down to look Koji in the face, "I would be with my ancestors at this very moment. I want to join them, but the later the better." As he straightened up, he chuckled with his hand over his mouth.

Again Papa bowed to Tanaka Shinzaemon. "I'm glad my humble son was able to help you," he said proudly.

Mama threw a straw rain cape over Koji and

pushed him out the door. He set off unwillingly, splashing through the mud to keep up with the master dye maker's strides. Once he glanced over his shoulder at his house. Under the dripping eaves, Taro stood alone, his teeth clamped on his lower lip as he watched Koji go.

At least my going protects Taro, Koji thought, *whether he knows it or not.* He turned and ran ahead through the pouring rain.

C
H
A
P
T
E
R

2

n a sunny afternoon a few moons later, Koji stood in the large garden of the master dye maker's rambling house. He broke a cherry branch in two, then stuck both pieces through his sash like swords worn at his hip. Puffing out his silk kimono, he admired his shadow with the long and short sticks extending behind him. *That's what I'd look like if I were a samurai warrior with two swords,* he thought.

Leaning against the cherry tree, he crossed one ankle over the other. But he kept his hand on the hilt of his stick-sword. Whistling under his breath, he pretended he was relaxing when . . .

Aha! Yanking the longer stick out of his sash, he spun around, imagining a *ninja* jumping him from behind. But he stopped short as the master dye maker's mother, old Obaasan, stepped out of the house onto the wooden walkway that connected the house, fireproof storage hut, and dye shop. She peered at the Zen courtyard with its sand-covered plot, raked to resemble ocean waves. "Kojiro!" She scowled at the stone lantern and each ornamental rock, as if he might be hiding behind one of them.

She squinted beyond the courtyard at the groomed garden laid out within the earthen wall. She was peering dangerously near Koji, and he dropped, like a felled warrior, behind a gnarled pine tree that loomed over the garden pond. He'd feared Obaasan since he'd first met her and she'd shaken her fist, shouting, "Scrawny farm rats are unwelcome in my son's house! I never gave my permission for you to come!"

Then and now, he tried hard to please his foster parents. He even enjoyed plunging his hands into the slippery blue dye in the deep dye pots. But Obaasan! His first few days here, he had labored hard over the chores she gave him. But each time, she only sniffed at his finished work. Finally, Koji gave up trying to satisfy her.

Staying out of Obaasan's sight, Koji crawled behind bushes onto the garden footbridge over the pond. One glimpse of him and Obaasan would start in on how useless he was, perhaps even hitting him with that long bamboo-and-ivory pipe tucked under her *obi*. But hidden here on the stone footbridge, he was safe.

A wooden bucket stood nearby. Earlier, he'd filled it with weeds. As he gazed at them, sudden panic made the back of his neck prickly. How had drooping peonies come to be stuck up alongside the weeds' mud-caked roots? He had been daydreaming of home while he weeded the flower bed. Had unhappiness made him so reckless that he'd torn up as many flowers as weeds?

Koji imagined Obaasan's face going as white as raw fish when she saw the dead blossoms. She would tear his hair out of his scalp. How did he manage always to blunder things with her?

Although . . . Koji blinked up into the sun as a trace of hope slipped between his fears. The sting of Obaasan's pipe, *if* she could catch him, was a small price to pay if it meant that she ordered her son to send Koji back home. The possibility had pressed in on him before, but he'd always pushed it away and resolved to keep trying to fit in. Now his shoulders sagged. He missed home—Mama, Papa, and the twin nobody here knew he had.

He looked away from the bucket of flowers and weeds, squared his shoulders, and tried to think cheerier thoughts. His stomach felt pleasantly cold against the stone footbridge, and a few plum petals drifted down onto his hair. He dipped his hand, blue-fingered from stirring the dye, into the pond. He grabbed at the swimming carp. They flickered as he snatched at them, one after another. Sometimes a fingertip grazed a slippery fish, but more often not.

After pulling his hand out of the water, he gazed at the inscription carved into the stone footbridge. The story went that one day when the master dye maker's grandfather was young, a fortuneteller predicted that the someru-ya was doomed to chronic bad luck. The master dye maker's grandfather spent the whole night chiseling these words into this footbridge, keeping his family awake with the *chink! chink! chink!*

True enough, once the sun rose on the inscription, "Good luck abides here," the someru-ya had begun to thrive. It had continued to do so until the man's grandson, now master dye maker in his own right, took steps to adopt a farm boy, Kojiro. *Poor, tricked man,* Koji thought. *If he'd hired Taro, as he intended, things would definitely be going better for him.*

Again Koji splashed his hand underwater to get a carp, and again he failed. With his mouth twisted in frustration, he stared hard at the passing fish. It didn't really matter whether he caught one, yet it did matter to him, not because of the fish but because of something about himself.

He set his determination to the task, held his breath, narrowed his eyes, and . . . There! He snapped his hand around the thin back of a white-and-orange-spotted carp. For a moment, he gently gripped the narrow sides of the fish while it struggled to swim free. As he released his fingers, a victory grin spread across his face.

He pulled his hand out of the water to see whether his blue fingers were slimy. Rolling onto his shoulder to get a good look, he went too far, lost his balance, and splashed into the dark pond.

He hit bottom, bounced up sputtering, and floundered the few steps back to the footbridge. Through the water streaming down his face, he stared at the good-luck inscription. Every single day, Obaasan rubbed her hand over the carved characters, praying, "Stay with us, luck." Whenever she caught Koji pulling the moss out of the chiseled grooves, she screamed.

He had meant to stop, but this footbridge was where he always hid when he felt homesick. Inevitably, his fingers would begin to pick, pick, pick at the moss. Now he saw that while his head and heart were busy missing home, his worried fingers had scraped clean every last character that Obaasan prized.

Koji's guilty glance traveled from the inscription to the drooping peony heads peeping out of the bucket, then up at the house. Obaasan had stopped searching for him. She stood among the indigo-encrusted dye pots and hung pieces of freshly dyed cloth.

Hoisting himself out of the pond, Koji was startled. Two broad feet stood planted on the muddy bank. Above them Koji saw strong, widely spread legs, gnarled fists on hips, and a broad chest. The master dye maker's thick neck made him look bullish at the best of times. Now, glaring down at the freshly picked characters on the footbridge, his face was all downturned mouth and frowning brow.

"Please remove that bucket of weeds," the master dye maker said as the boy clambered to his feet. Then, as he leaned forward to peer at the uprooted peonies, his frown deepened. "Can't you tell Obaasan's flowers from weeds?" he growled. "Isn't it enough that you pick at the moss she wants left alone?"

To steel himself against crying, Koji held his breath and stared hard at the bits of moss littering the ground. But air burst out of him in a loud *bupp!* When he peeped up at the master dye maker's face, it was tight with anger. Koji realized with dismay that the man thought he had laughed. He wanted to speak, to explain, to defend himself, but he felt as hollow and wordless as a dried gourd.

"Leave it. The moss and flowers will grow back after you're gone."

Koji shot a glance at the man's tight jaw. Gone?

"When you helped me on the riverbank, Koji, I thought you would be thrilled to become my apprentice. I don't often misjudge people, but this time I did. You're too homesick to function here." He picked up the bucket of peonies. "I've given you one more chance, then one more, then one more again. But you will never fit into this family. I'm sending you home."

Only a few minutes ago, Koji had toyed with the thought of how glad he would be to leave the someruya. But now he realized what it would be like to arrive home: the stunned disappointment in his parents' eyes, their regret that they hadn't sent Taro here as they should have, their shock turning to shame as he confessed why he had been sent home.

Taro will understand, though, he thought. *I'll tell him, not them, my side of the story. Then I'll let him do all my explaining.* What luck to have Taro always in reserve!

He rubbed his sweaty hands up and down along the sides of his kimono. But noticing disapproval in the master dye maker's face, he clasped his hands against his stomach instead. He tightened his locked fingers to stop them from wriggling, sucked in his very Koji-ness, pushed it down.

He couldn't control himself for another moment. "I don't want to shame my family!" he cried, flinging himself on the ground and pressing his forehead into the dirt. It was the deepest bow he could make, yet when he looked up, the master dye maker was already plodding away. Koji scrambled up and ran after him with his hands still clasped. "Please don't send me home, Honorable Foster Father! I'll behave, I promise!"

The master dye maker didn't turn. "Promises, little man."

"Pleasepleaseplease!"

"Perhaps in another year you will have matured," the master dye maker said over his shoulder.

"So you'll give me another chance in a year?" Koji called. It would console his parents, and next year seemed far away.

The master dye maker kept walking, up the path past the *ai* seedlings, freshly planted to make indigo dye.

Koji let his pleading hands fall. He trailed after the man, his chest heaving with suppressed tears. "By next year, you will have found a different boy to be your apprentice," he moaned. The master dye maker didn't answer. He didn't turn or even glance back, and feeling sick, Koji realized that arguing was hopeless. He must go home.

oster Mother knelt next to Koji on the *tatami* mat. She was wrapping a few things for him in an indigo cloth he'd helped dye. "So you blame all your mischief on Obaasan?" she asked, summing up all he had just said in a rush. "Koji, you must learn to yield to your elders." She paused before adding, "Did your naughtiness have nothing to do with missing home?"

Koji stuck out his lower lip and crossed his arms. *How wonderful it must feel to be Taro,* he thought. *Taro always knows what to do with his hands. And Mama and Papa kept him instead of me.*

"Are you a wild monkey, not to answer when spoken to? Obaasan bosses me as much as you. I suffer but hold my tongue."

"You? Suffer?"

"I used to wish Obaasan would stop ordering me

around. But once I realized that she is bossy by nature, I accepted that she'll never stop." She tipped her head, considering him. "Looking at you has caused a poem to leap into my mind.

Fine cloth in blue hands
A journey before twilight
One tear on his cheek.

"Will you remember my poem?" she asked, stroking Koji's bundle.

"Yes," Koji promised, although he'd forgotten it already. He found wealthy people's poem-making ways odd. If his mother stood up in the rice paddy and recited a poem while mud streamed from her hands, she would look like a fool. "I thought poetry had to be about cherry blossoms and pines and the moon," he said.

"Some people say emotions should never be expressed except through poetry, and even then only on certain topics. But I believe poetry may be about anything that evokes emotion." Foster Mother's face was impassive, but her hands trembled. "And this day, Koji, you have evoked mine."

Koji didn't know what to say. He'd learned that in fine homes like this one, vague discussions were polite and clear talk, rude. When he spoke, he must always blur his meanings. His foster parents had a hundred rules. He must glide and never skip. Keep his hands down at his sides. Stay in the main parts of the sprawling house and dye shop. The kind of exploring he and

Taro loved was unacceptable here. Most of all, he must never speak his mind plainly.

But he was only a farm boy, confused by formal ways. "Will you stay patient forever?" he asked Foster Mother.

"Of course." She pulled tight two corners of the cloth wrapping, knotted them over the other two, and handed the bundle to Koji. "Please tell your mother that the rice cakes with bean paste are a special treat for your homecoming dinner."

"Thank you. I do want to go back to Mama," Koji admitted. He reached inside his kimono and touched the Jizo Mama had given him. He kept it next to his heart.

Foster Mother smiled. "I've also packed some pine nuts. I'm sorry the gift is so small and unworthy."

"It's a wonderful gift. And I'm not crying," he added, covering his eyes with his arm. "But my parents will hate me."

"Of course not." Foster Mother reached out and lowered Koji's arm from in front of his face. "Even your foster father likes you. But he has a business to run and no time for disorder."

Koji folded his hands, trying to behave in the refined way she craved from him. He blinked through tears trapped in his eyelashes. "What will my parents say when I walk in?"

"Were they proud of you when you came to the dye shop?"

Koji didn't answer, knowing it was Taro who had

earned this position at the someru-ya. "At home, I'll be another mouth. Lord Udo's rice tax is so high. He always takes almost all of our crop, with no thought for us. If this year's crop is bad, he'll take every grain of our rice. We'll starve!"

"I'm sorry that's how things are, Koji, but I have no power to change your life or my own. Your foster father knows what's best for the someru-ya, and his mind is made up. You must go home." She slid open the paper door and stepped out onto the wooden walkway. In the garden beyond the raked sand of the Zen courtyard, the gnarled pine tree stood out against a hazy backdrop. "Foggy up in the mountains," she murmured, gazing off.

Koji had a sudden idea. "Honorable Foster Mother, may I leave tomorrow instead?" he asked, still kneeling, clutching the bundle she'd given him. With one more day, he felt sure he could wheedle the master dye maker into letting him stay.

"My honorable husband wishes to finish with this dilemma now, and to sleep free of worry tonight. But surely there's good in seeing your parents this very day?"

"I've disgraced them," Koji said, moaning. But Foster Mother had no more comfort to give him, so he bowed and started out. He nearly bumped into the master dye maker, bull-necked and filling the doorway. The man held his arms straight out with a short length of cloth, wrapped in rice paper, draped over his hands.

"A gift for your father," he said.

Koji lifted the paper to get a better look. "For my father?" he asked, baffled. "But it has a crane pattern."

"I know. It is unworthy, poorly dyed, and small," the man said politely, though the cloth was beautiful.

"Just the opposite, Honorable Foster Father," Koji said, remembering at the last moment to bow. "Isn't this Udo-sama's personal design, made only by the someru-ya? My humble father has no right to possess a piece of a samurai's cloth."

"Udo-sama would agree, but I want to send it home with you. Your father can keep it secretly hidden in the cupboard under his altar. Perhaps he'll go easy on you, bringing such a thing."

Respectfully, Koji touched the cloth to his forehead.

From behind Koji, Foster Mother murmured, "Honorable Husband, if you start home with him now, you'll be back here before dusk."

The man seized Koji's arm and guided him outside.

"I can get myself home," Koji muttered, wriggling.

The master dye maker's grip tightened. "No, little man. What I start, I finish. But first, a goodbye to Obaasan."

Koji hung back as the man guided him around the house toward the place where Obaasan often went to hang lengths of dyed cloth. She had a way of swishing her kimono as she moved, and when Koji heard the familiar sound, his face flamed up in anger. Something happened in his throat, a sort of pounding and sour taste. *I'm not homesick,* he told himself as she came into view. *It's all Obaasan's fault that I've shamed my family.*

Koji tore out of the man's grip. He yanked his kimono up to his knees, leaped off the walkway, and dashed across the Zen courtyard. His heels dug wounds into the manicured sand.

Behind him, he heard the master dye maker running, *slap slap slap* on the walkway. "Koji!" he cried. "Stop! Come back!"

But Koji kept sprinting. Foster Mother and Obaasan shouted from behind, too, but respectful of the groomed sand, they stayed on the walkway with the master dye maker. Dashing at an angle across the sand, Koji charged around the stone lantern. He darted into the garden and, hidden behind the gnarled pine tree, slid into the pond.

Awkwardly holding his bundle and piece of cloth out of the water, he splashed toward the shadow under the footbridge. When he was hidden, he squeezed the two things onto the patch of dry earth between the underside of the footbridge and the water's edge. Then he raised his head so that his eyes and ears were just above the water, level with the floating lotus leaves.

Soon feet made noise on the footbridge overhead. "The gate's open. He must have set out alone." Foster Mother sounded distressed.

"Why wouldn't he want me to go with him to explain?" the master dye maker asked.

"Perhaps, Honorable Husband, he fears what you might say."

Obaasan, with her distinctive, shuffling footsteps, joined them on the footbridge. "What are you planning?" she snapped.

"The boy has run home," the master dye maker muttered.

"Hurry, Husband, please go after him!"

"I suppose I better follow him home. After all, I still need to explain the situation to his father."

Obaasan made a hissing sound. "Good riddance!"

"Ah, now," the man said. "He's only a child."

Obaasan snorted. "A useless one!"

Koji lowered his head under the silent water and squinted up at the water line. When he raised his head, Foster Mother was telling Obaasan, "Yes. Yes. Of course. Yes."

Koji looked up at the footbridge overhead. Foster Mother had told him to behave as she did toward Obaasan. Was this yes, yes, yessing what she meant? *Never,* Koji thought, clenching his jaw. *Never.*

"Please stop wasting time," Foster Mother urged. Koji heard the master dye maker grunt and stride off the footbridge.

Koji peeked out from the shadow. He watched the women start toward the house together. Obaasan's back was rigid, and now and then she swatted Foster Mother with the bowl of her pipe. Foster Mother walked like a bamboo bent against high winds.

espite Koji's efforts, both the crane cloth and the bundle were damp. He scrambled out of the pond and did his best to dry them. Then, dripping wet for the second time that day, he slipped out through the someru-ya's open wicker gateway. He felt a surprising pang once he was outside the earthen wall, but he held his breath and pushed down regret. Then he started home.

He had an idea. He would take shortcuts, arrive at his house before the master dye maker got there, then crawl under the raised farmhouse. Once he'd heard the man's speech and his parents' reaction, he would find Taro and together they would plan his excuses.

Feeling a glimmer of hope after a shattering day, Koji left the road. He crossed the ten flooded rice paddies that stretched along the valley. His family's field was the nearest one to the scattering of thatched cottages that made up Kurikawa village and, beyond it, Aokusai. In the paddy next to his family's, he knelt behind the stick-and-rag scarecrow hung with bits of wood that rattled when the wind blew. Longingly, he watched Papa and Taro at work in the field. Wearing identical loincloths and headbands, they stood up to their ankles in water. Taro plucked weeds from between the rows of rice shoots. Papa wet his hands with irrigation water that flowed through bamboo tubes, then patted mud onto the crumbling dirt wall between his rice field and the next one.

Mama came shuffling along the raised wall between the paddies. Wearing a conical straw hat over a kerchief tied under her chin, she carried a tray of rice cakes and melon for the family's meal. Koji longed to see her face, but she was looking down at the tray, and her face was hidden.

Seeing his family, Koji felt as if the Jizo next to his heart was on fire. *But do they love me back?* he wondered. All his life they had farmed by his side. When he tired, they took the hoe from him and dragged it through the earth with their own hands. And after angry arguments, peace always returned.

Each move Taro made was a miniature of their father's—the way he snapped his wrist to toss away a weed, even the way he stretched. Everyone in the village said it was so. But no one had ever said Koji moved like Papa. Also, there had been that odd look between their parents, just before . . .

Koji clenched his teeth. No. He would not let himself wonder why they'd sent him away in his brother's place. He couldn't wait to take off this brocade kimono and dress comfortably, like Papa and Taro. It would feel good to share miso soup with his family tonight, and he could count on Taro to deflect his parents' wrath.

When Mama reached the paddy, she stood talking and plucking out weeds. Papa and Taro squatted on the embankment between the fields and wolfed down their meals. Koji longed to throw himself in among them before they finished up their day's work and set out for Kurikawa. But he still needed to beat both them and the master dye maker home.

He tucked his kimono up between his legs and into his sash. Taking back paths, he raced all the way home to the thatched farmhouse of paper-covered walls and flimsy, wood-framed doors. He pushed the cloth and bundle deep into the pocket formed by his overlapping lapels. Then he flung himself down beside the house, slid under the raised floor, and scooted along on his back until he thought he was near the hearth, where Papa was sure to receive the master dye maker. From here, Koji knew he would be able to hear their conversation.

The air under the house was thick and stuffy. Mosquitoes buzzed around him, and his damp and dirty kimono itched. But none of that mattered. Koji was home . . . home. He turned his face toward the dirt, closed his eyes, and sniffed. The earth of Kurikawa had its own special smell, a smell fresher than the dirt near the dye shop. The scent of that dirt was hardly notice-able above the heavy aroma of dyes in the air. But this soil had a strong, vital smell.

He put his hands under the back of his head like a pillow and heaved a sigh. *My troubles at the someru-ya were about homesickness,* he realized. But all that was behind him. He was home now. Home, where moonlight peeped through holes in the thatched roof under which he had been born. Home, where next to him slept his brother, the exact image of himself. Home, where Amida Buddha knew to send blessings to him. . . .

He woke suddenly, tried to sit up, and soundlessly bumped his head on the floor of the house. Hearing muffled voices above, he remembered where he was.

Straining upward, he heard the master dye maker say, "Can't fit in . . . My mother . . . " and his father mumble, ". . . did teach him respect, but . . . shames us." Then the master dye maker again: ". . . immature . . . too spirited . . . impolite . . ."

And at last, Papa's single, chilling word: ". . . dis-grace . . ."

The master dye maker's feet in *tabi* appeared out-side the door. The feet slipped into geta that were still dark where Koji had splashed water on them when he climbed out of the pond.

Koji stared up at the bit of rush matting visible between the floorboards overhead. He'd left the someru-ya knowing he'd shamed his family. Even so, his face burned over his father's unthinkable word—

disgrace. What if Papa's anger and shame never ceased?

He heard his mother crossing the floor above him. Soon he could see her feet near the door, facing out, as if she were looking down the road. "But where is he?"

"Coming along . . . dawdling . . . ," Papa muttered.

"I don't see him," she insisted. "Oh, he must arrive."

"Any minute he will," Papa reassured her.

Papa's voice came from a spot directly above Koji, who scowled and squirmed away. When the floorboards overhead creaked again, he slid away for a second time. Little by little, he was moving toward the opening out from under the house.

"Koji!" He glanced over to find Taro under the house with him and crawling closer. After a day in the rice paddies, Taro's hair hung in sweaty strings. But never had he worn a wider smile. "Why are you home?" he asked in a thrilled rush.

Shame stiffened Koji's cheeks like new leather. He'd been so eager to see Taro, but now Papa had said that word, *disgrace.* Would Taro agree?

Taro's smile faded. "What's wrong?" he asked, then sudden hope sprang up in his face. "Did the master dye maker let you come home for a visit?"

Koji wiped tears off his cheeks. "Let me by!"

"Tell me what's wrong!"

"Shh. They'll know I'm here."

"Why shouldn't they?"

Koji couldn't make his mouth move to answer. But

his fingers kept frantically clawing up gritty dirt, then sifting it onto the ground and clawing up more.

Taro stared at Koji's fidgeting hand. "Oh, no," Taro murmured, his voice trailing off. When he continued speaking, his slow words were cold. "He *sent* you away. You ruined your chance."

"Taro, will you talk to Mama and Papa for me and—"

"*Our* chance. How could you? One chance at life between the two of us. I wanted it, Koji, but I gave it up for you. And now you've thrown it all away!"

"But Taro, I didn't mean—"

Taro scooped up a handful of dirt. He flung it in Koji's face.

With a trembling hand, Koji reached up to touch his cheek. Yes, he felt dirt there, so it was true. Never had Taro done anything like this. *Everyone hates me,* Koji thought. *Even Taro.*

"Oh, Koji," Taro groaned. "If you knew how much hope Papa and Mama had for you! It's been like . . . like all our lives changed, like the whole family shared your one chance. Every night, in front of the altar—"

"But I couldn't help it. I missed all of you and—"

"What? You ruined our lives over homesickness? Big baby!"

Koji pulled himself up at the side of the house and crouched to avoid being seen. His chest was heaving. "Taro, don't tell them you saw me," he begged.

"Why not?" Taro, still on the ground, grabbed Koji's ankle. "You're not going off somewhere else?"

"Yes, I . . ." Then he had a brilliant idea. "You've misunderstood everything! I'm here because . . . because I'm on an errand. See?" He pulled the crane cloth from inside his kimono and waved it at Taro. "Cloth from the someru-ya. But I have to get back right away. The master dye maker needs me and . . . and he wants me. Very much!"

"You mean, you haven't ruined things after all?" Taro asked, looking relieved as he scrambled to his feet. "Then why did you say it? A joke like that would break Mama's and Papa's hearts."

Koji didn't answer. Never had he known that shame is a pair of rocks, one that sits in your stomach and the other in your throat. Finally, he whispered, "I never want to break their hearts."

"No. Phew! What luck that you tried out your bad joke on me first. Sorry I threw dirt at you. I didn't mean to, I just . . . Come see. I'm making you a present. So far, it looks like an eggplant, but if I can whittle well enough, I'm going to turn it into a boat."

"Of course you can whittle well enough to turn an eggplant into a boat. Taro, don't you know you can do anything?"

"I don't know about that! You're the strong one," he added, squeezing Koji's bicep. "But—"

Koji didn't wait to hear what Taro had to say. He turned and ran. Maybe Taro called him back. Maybe he followed. Koji didn't know. He ran too fast to know. He ran away from Taro, away from Papa and Mama, even away from himself. His legs had a will of their own. Without knowing where he was going, he struck out up a hillside of terraced rice paddies. As he ran, a fog began to grow. Those two rocks of sorrow had worked themselves upward and were now behind his eyes, making them sting.

The mist thickened as Koji trudged higher. He would hide in its embrace until nighttime—the hour of the dog. Surely it would be easier to face his parents after dark, when the shadows of candlelight masked the brokenhearted looks on their faces.

Perhaps in the dim light they wouldn't realize that his heart was broken as well.

t twilight, Koji stood alone, wrapped in fog as dense as a silkworm's cocoon. If only he'd faced out the horror at home, he'd be safe at his own hearth now, and the hearts he'd broken would already be starting to mend. Instead, misty tendrils slithered down his back. He squinted, looking for landmarks, but only bamboo trees surrounded him. Scared and aching for home, he longed for that half-whittled boat. He wanted to thank Taro for it and to cradle it in his hand. With all Taro's carving ability, he had never made such a thing even for himself.

Koji would rather have faced Papa's worst scolding than a night in the dark forest, alone. *How could I have stumbled into such a mess?* he wondered. *I must have passed a fox, and it put a curse on me.* He licked his finger and wet his eyebrows for protection.

Countless times, Papa had warned him not to

stray into this bamboo grove. "*Tengu* live in there, Kojiro," he had said. "Winged ones with long noses and bulging eyes that ooze slime. They have sharp claws instead of fingernails, and they'll dig those claws into you and throw you down into hell! Promise me you'll never go in among those bamboos!"

Koji promised, then and the thousand other times when that worried look came into his father's eyes. Of course he didn't want to be caught by tengu! He meant his promise with all his heart.

Yet here he was, lost in the hushed prison of bamboo trunks, dark bars in a lighter haze. He reached out as if he were blind and crept through the drizzle. Damp creepers brushed against his arms like the trailing fingers of evil spirits. The night was endless.

Ghostly vines looped between ancient trees. Koji kept trying to turn around and head down the mountain, but always the ground would slope upward again. Step by wrong step, he was hiking high into the steep, rugged mountains.

It occurred to him that maybe the fog didn't extend too high above the ground. If he could get a look over the forest, perhaps he could see a route down into the valley. He dropped his bundle and the crane cloth on the ground. With his heart pounding hard, he began climbing an oak. Did winged tengu stay close to the earth, or did they fly around up high?

He groped upward through the fog as he climbed, finding branch after branch to grab on to and lift himself higher. But one time when he reached out, instead of touching a branch, he gripped a blade. It was too rusted and dull to cut him, but it was a blade nevertheless. He pulled his hand away as if he'd been burned.

A blade way up in a tree?

It was too weird. Big-eyed, he stretched to get a look at what he hoped was only an oddly sharp branch, and at last he drew close enough to see it through the fog. An ancient sword extended horizontally through the trunk, as if it were part of the tree. It was old, but definitely steel. The hilt grew out of the far side of the trunk and the blade stretched out above Koji. Had it been placed there, long ago, to hurt anyone who tried to climb this tree?

He was horrified, and without looking over the forest, he descended as fast as he could. On the ground, he gathered up his cloth and bundle and had staggered only a few yards before a mossy boulder appeared like a ninja warrior leaping out of the fog. Koji collapsed against it to wait for morning.

As he stared into the fog streaked with eerie stripes, Koji nervously folded and refolded the crane cloth. What if Taro thought he had meant to run away from home and told their parents that? Could you break someone's heart twice? Could you break people's hearts so badly that they didn't want to see you ever again, not even if you were their own son?

He looked around at the foggy shadows. Were wolves watching him with their long tongues hanging down over needle teeth? He remembered hearing of a boy who had disappeared from the valley. Papa said he'd wandered into the tengu's bamboo forest on the mountain and been snatched away. But Mama thought animals had devoured him.

Sitting against the boulder, Koji opened the bundle from Foster Mother and gulped down what little food he had. "All of Kurikawa will search for me tomorrow," he said timidly to the night, and was reassured to hear sound, even his own whisper. He clenched his jaw, then cleared his throat and spoke out bravely. "Everyone from Aokusai will come, too. Mama and Papa will lead them all, running for me with their arms out. It will be sunny and Taro will bring my boat, all finished." He fell silent but hated the silence and added, "We'll have a picnic on straw mats. Under the trees. With rice cakes and tea and all my favorite foods."

From within the desolate forest, an owl hooted. Koji realized how damp his kimono and hair had become from the fog. Dizzy with exhaustion, he eyed the ghostly stripes all around and grabbed a heavy branch to guard against tengu and wolves. *Don't fall asleep!* he thought. *Don't fall asleep . . . don't fall asleep . . .*

A black shape struck him across the chest. A tengu! Even half asleep, Koji's reflexes were fast. He fought his way free, but the shape was like a sucker fish. It held him down. It punched. It kicked. Koji's flailing arms were useless.

The shape lay over Koji. A gag was clapped down over his mouth. Sharp claws cut his cheek. He tasted his own blood. His muscles went limp and his lungs emptied. Colors floated before his eyes. As he started to black out, he felt the crane cloth slip from his fingers.

The tengu snatched away the cloth over Koji's mouth, and he managed to get one more breath. A dagger flashed in the moonlight and cold steel pressed against his neck. "Feel my knife? Who are you?"

Koji hesitated, and the creature flicked its fingers against his ribs as if to warn him that it would stab Koji there. The touch was even more horrible for being so tender. Yet it cleared Koji's mind. Using all his strength, he wrenched away and drove his fist into the tengu's stomach.

But the tengu seemed to fly over Koji's head. It landed behind him. Koji scrambled up. Something exploded in his face. He fell. His nose throbbed and bled. The tengu flung him down again, and again the blade pressed on his neck, this time in front where his blood pulsated hard.

"I asked, who are you?"

"Farm boy!" Koji choked out.

"What are you doing here?"

"Lost!"

"Don't move even one toe." The cold blade slid away. Koji heard flint strike steel. Sparks sprang up and a flame appeared off a sliver of wood. It was held by a hand wearing a dark, fingerless glove.

The flame illuminated the crane cloth, then was snuffed. Koji's enemy jerked the fabric away. "Udo-sama's crane cloth. You're from Crane Castle!"

"Go away, tengu!"

"Get up!" said the shape, all black except for a pair of eyes. A cord whipped out of the fog. Koji's captor forced his arms behind him, then looped the cord around his crossed thumbs and tied his wrists together. "See this?" The enemy held out a star-shaped piece of steel that glinted in the moonlight. "If you run, I'll sink it into your skull." He slapped Koji on the top of the head. "Forward! Go!"

hey clambered over tree roots and craggy rocks to climb even higher into the foggy mountains. Koji's captor sometimes shoved him and sometimes pressed a knife point against his back to make him go forward. More than once, he held Koji back while he whistled like a *hototogisu* bird. Each time, he was answered by the same call. Koji felt as if a flock of invisible birds was escorting them into a nightmare.

Eventually, the forest opened into a large clearing lit here and there by bonfires. The fires had dispelled the fog and shed dim light over a broad field of trampled grass, dirt paths, and a few bushes and trees. Ropes hung coiled around tree trunks and were strung overhead. The field ended at a high cliff covered with wisteria vines.

Two men sat talking beside the closest fire. One poked a stick at sweet potatoes roasting in the ashes.

The other blew at the flame through a short piece of bamboo. As Koji's captor pushed him forward into the clearing, the men leaped to their feet. Both looked ready to attack. One brandished a strange chain-and-rod contraption. The other did two high back flips in their direction. He landed in fighting stance with his hands up as if they were weapons.

Koji's captor stepped out from behind him. "Uncle Firefly, it's me—Spider!" he called.

Nodding, the man lowered his hands. Spider thrust Koji past both staring men toward the cliff at the back of the clearing. As Koji lurched closer, he expected Spider to push him left or right so that he wouldn't slam into the cliff. But he didn't. He kept shoving him forward, and the vine-covered rock face kept looming larger. Every crack, tuft of crabgrass, and wisteria flower stood out clearly.

At the last moment, Koji saw that, hidden behind the screen of vines, a narrow fissure opened into the cliff. Spider thrust him through it into a cave. The dank air hit him as his feet rasped on the gritty floor. Nearby, torches stood wedged into cracks in the cave walls. Their flickering light showed eerie shadows, and wisps of smoke rolled up from sticks of incense and hovered beneath the low, rounded ceiling. Farther back where there were no torches, the dark cave branched out into black slits in the rock walls.

Spider pushed Koji down onto his stomach on a ragged straw mat. Panting hard, Koji strained to look up over his shoulder and saw wicker baskets lining the walls, and gourds and bamboo ladles hanging from pegs nailed into cracks. A woven straw jacket was draped over a stone column. Hanging nets held jumbles of strange weapons made from chains, weights, and blades.

A man stepped over Koji and stood with one foot on either side of him. He gripped a curved sword. "Please!" Koji cried, but the man raised his sword anyway. Firelight glittered on its shiny surface as it hung poised, ready to split Koji in two.

Slash!

The sword sliced down exactly far enough to sever the cord that tied Koji's hands together. He jerked out of the broken binding and rubbed his aching wrists. One swift blow had not only cut the rope but had done it without even grazing his skin.

"Get up!"

As he clambered to his feet, someone entered the cave. "Blindfold the boy!" the person commanded in a voice that sounded as if a fish bone were caught in his throat.

Someone jerked Koji's head back and wrapped a blindfold over his eyes so tightly that his head throbbed.

"Boy, you have dared to venture into the forest of tengu," said the raspy voice. "Ve-e-e-r-y dangerous."

Koji's breath came hard. His instinct was still to attack. Yet he also wanted to roll up into a ball and cry. And, too, he knew that if his father were here, he would remind him that this was a time for bowing and crouching. And begging.

Instead of doing any of these, Koji shocked himself by blurting, "My father always warned me that tengu live on this mountain. But you aren't tengu. You're people."

A stunned silence. Then the raspy voice spoke again. It trembled with rage. "By now, this boy should be food for the vultures. You know that disobedience is punished by death. Shall I execute you with him?"

Execute him. Koji's beating pulse hurt his throat.

The raspy voice commanded, "Bear, take the boy . . ."

"But look!" Koji heard Spider beg.

The raspy voice was greedy now. "Let me see that." And after a pause, "Remove the boy's blindfold."

Someone yanked the murderously tight cloth off his face. Blessed relief. On the cave floor, an old man sat in full lotus position on a scarlet cushion. He had a skull-faced look, as if his skin was stretched too thin. His gray hair was drawn up into a scanty topknot, and the beard straggling down his chest was sparse. In front of him, tea things were set out on a rough wooden tray. With them stood a delicate bamboo cage the size of two teacups. It contained a mulberry leaf and one dark cricket. Lord Udo's crane cloth lay in the man's lap.

Koji scrambled to kneel with his forehead on the ground.

"Boy, what is your clan name?" The man sounded dangerous. His narrow eyes with too much eyelid looked reptilian.

"Clan? I'm no samurai's son, with a clan name. I

am an unworthy farm boy called Koji. I only got lost."

Frowning, the old man ran his hands over the crane cloth. "Why would a farm boy have Udo-sama's fabric?" He dropped the cloth and grazed the cricket cage with one finger until the cricket started chirping. "You're from the castle."

"Truly, I'm not."

"A warning—lies annoy me." With a piece of torn mat, he fanned the fire in the square wooden brazier lined with a clay box. Ashes fluttered up from the flames. The old man's hair was like ashes, too, the same color and just as dry. He motioned to someone behind him. "Remove these two."

"Dark Fire-sama, take away Spider, too?"

"I said two. Can you not count that high?"

rom behind, someone shoved Koji forward into a second dank cave. It was as dark as a bucket of the someru-ya's blackest dye. His legs were kicked out from under him. He lay shivering on the rock floor until someone was thrown down beside him. He realized it must be Spider. Fury struck him like a whirlwind. He lashed out. He clawed and hit. But Spider's body was a steel chain, flexible and strong. He easily forced Koji down and jerked his head back by the hair. Koji could have screamed from pain. He clenched his jaw instead and kept fighting.

"Quit punching me!" Spider said. "We're in the same mess now."

Koji was too enraged to speak. But in answer, he broke wind.

"You little . . . !" Spider began throttling him.

Koji's head bounced up and down against the rock floor. "Let me go!" he cried.

"Or what?" Spider sneered. He kneed Koji, who rolled onto his stomach and crawled away. When Koji struck the clammy cave wall, he jerked the stiff collar of his kimono up over his face.

Spider scrambled close. Even from inside his kimono, Koji could see that Spider had lit a flame beside him. "Go away," he said. He sounded scared and, feeling ashamed, he made fists.

Spider jerked Koji's head up out of his collar. Koji came up with his eyes squeezed shut. He smelled Spider's sour breath and felt the heat of the flame near his face.

"Open your eyes!"

Koji squeezed them tighter shut.

"I'll burn you if you don't."

Koji knew Spider wasn't bluffing. He opened his eyes. Spider was dressed all in blue-black: pants, jacket, and a hood with slits that showed sly little beady eyes under thick eyebrows.

The older boy flung the flaming sliver of wood into the air. Then with a twist, he flipped his star-shaped piece of steel at it. It whipped through the air so precisely that it struck the flame and put it out. Instantly, the cave went black. Koji heard the star drop into Spider's hand.

Spider made scrabbling noises. Koji guessed that he was crawling around the cave floor, sweeping together stray leaves and twigs. Flint struck steel again. Sparks. Tinder smoldered, and in no time a crackling fire lit the cave. It flared so quickly that it seemed magical.

Spider leaned over the flame and blew at it.

Koji stared at him, filled with fascination and terror and rage. Thanks to Spider, every inch of him hurt. "Who are you people?"

Taking his time, Spider untied his gloves and warmed his hands over the fire. Against his dark clothes, his uncovered hands hovered in the dim light as if they were disembodied. "Who are we?" he mused. "You could say we're watchers. When you think you're alone, we are there spying on you . . . invisible, but there." He pulled off the long piece of cloth that formed his hood, then shook his head as if throwing off water. He looked about fifteen. His narrow face was handsome, except for too heavy eyebrows. "Think of me as a blade of grass."

"Dumb riddle. What did I do to bother you?"

Spider tilted his chin up arrogantly. "You entered my forest. That bothered me."

All the fight seeped out of Koji. "Can't you—or somebody—help me find my way back down the mountain?" When Spider didn't answer, he added, "Will they really kill me?"

Spider sat down and clasped his arms around his knees. He stared at the fire as if in a trance. His silence was an answer.

Softly, Koji asked, "Soon?"

Still Spider didn't speak.

Koji placed both hands on his knees and stared down at them. "Will they do the same thing to you because you let me live?"

"Don't talk about it."

Koji buried his face in his hands. He had heard plenty of glorious stories about samurai who took their own lives rather than face dishonor. Was it true that they felt no fear of death? Fear made Koji's hands sweat.

Spider scrambled over to him. "You really can't guess who we are?" he murmured, as if death hadn't been mentioned at all.

Koji looked at Spider's strange dark clothes. He recalled the game he'd played at the someru-ya, of being jumped by a ninja. Was it possible that . . . ? But some villagers claimed that the ninja outcasts were supernatural beings, while Koji was sure Spider and the old man were people. "I can't guess."

"I'll give you a hint." Spider sprang into a back flip. Landing near the flames, he flashed a grin at Koji. Then, with a flamboyant sweep of his arm, he extracted from within his clothes an egg with a wax stopper at one end. He bit out the stopper, then turned the egg upside down. From it, he sprinkled powder into the flame. Blue sparks jumped up.

Crack!

As smoke puffed out of the fire, Koji turned away, coughing. When he swung back to the fire, Spider was gone.

Koji stared, only realizing after a few minutes that his mouth hung open. "Was that the hint?" he asked the darkness.

He was answered by his own echo.

The black cavern was filled with looming shadows and lonely, dripping sounds. "Come back!" Koji cried as the weak fire went out. He crawled around the edges of the black cave and ran his hands over the rough wall. Spider must have slipped through a crack, and Koji wanted to slip through it, too. But he couldn't find one. This cave's only opening was the entrance, and now it was blocked by two guards' broad backs. Yet Spider had vanished.

Koji was terrified to be without Spider, whom he thought of as both his enemy and his only friend. And was his family searching madly for him? Or had he disgraced himself so completely that they were glad to be rid of him?

He curled up on the cold rock floor and stared into the darkness, aching to relive the day, make different decisions. He would not let homesickness overcome him so that his anxious fingers pulled up peonies with weeds, then picked at moss while his mind daydreamed. He would let the master dye maker walk him home, or he would at least tell Taro the truth, then beg him for advice. Most of all, he would stay in Kurikawa and not run away.

He had barely nodded off before he was hoisted onto sleep-wobbly legs and thrust out into a new day. He stood, rubbing his scratchy eyes. Two guards talked behind him, one gripping his shoulder. The air smelled of millet and fish cooking.

"Can I have something to eat?" Koji asked timidly, for he'd eaten nothing since he'd wolfed down the provisions from Foster Mother in the forest the night before.

The guard shook Koji's shoulder. "You eat when we say so."

The cave faced the open area that Koji had seen in the night. He made a rough count of a hundred people in the clearing—more than lived in Kurikawa. Children bustled around, grouped by age. One or two adults oversaw each bunch. Koji was amazed. At home, males and females had different roles. But here everyone worked together.

And what strange things they were doing. On one side, older boys and girls took turns punching man-shaped straw forms, their hands making soft *thunks*. Occasionally, one of them back-flipped toward the dummies from some distance and, while in midair, lifted his foot over his head and knocked the dummy down.

Children of four or five were sword fighting with sticks. As they dueled, they somersaulted, leaped, and flipped. The clatter of the branch-swords sounded like play, but the babyish faces were deadly serious.

Boys sprinted to a thick wooden post, then let their momentum carry them straight up it. At the top, they would flip their legs over their heads and jump down. Near them, some girls watched a woman draw a long, dangerous hairpin out of her elaborate coiffure and lunge forward to stab with it.

Koji tried to pull away from the guards, but they gripped him tightly. He could hardly believe his own stupidity: taking Taro's chance from him, then throwing it away, and now winding up in this strange place. *Everyone who knows me must hate me,* he thought. *How can they help it? I hate myself.*

A boy about Spider's age ran zigzagging through the groups to make an abrupt halt before Koji. "Hello!" he cried, grinning.

"Uh, hello," Koji said cautiously as he watched a girl leap over a thorny vine suspended between two stumps. She slashed her leg on the thorns and hobbled away, gushing blood—but not crying.

"You're from the village?" the smiling boy asked Koji.

"Falcon," said the guard behind Koji, "this boy has nothing to do with you."

"But he comes from the valley, and I want to talk to him," Falcon said. "You know—"

"Go train, Falcon!"

Reluctantly, Falcon turned and lifted two bags of stones onto his shoulders, then cast a quick, almost longing smile at Koji before sprinting around the edges of the open area. Others running with him pressed straw hats against their chests and ran fast enough to prevent the hats from falling. Above them, children moved hand over hand along ropes.

Koji's body tightened with shock as he noticed the strangest sight of all. To one side, a woman knelt over gurgling infants laid out on a bearskin. At first they were all sleeping or flapping their hands happily. But working with one child at a time, she rocked a tiny arm or leg until the delicate bone dislodged from its joint. As that baby started screaming, the woman would move on to the next child, leaving the puny body unjointed for several minutes before replacing the bone.

As he watched, horrified, Koji was shoved forward again. Soon he stood in the cave where he'd been taken the night before. He blinked while his eyes adjusted to the dim light. As before, the raspy-voiced old man called Dark Fire sat in front of the brazier. From within the cricket cage beside him, his little pet chirped as a guard put down a cushion for Koji to kneel on. Remembering an extremely polite gesture Mama had taught him, he knelt beside the cushion instead of on it.

A look of surprised approval crossed the old man's face. "When you arrived here last night, you guessed that we are not tengu, but people. Anyone suspecting such a thing might be wise to keep silent about it, don't you think?" The man's eyes were cold. "Tell me, what people are we?"

"Well, in Kurikawa, the villagers sometimes said . . . ," Koji began. Then confusion and fear sealed his lips.

"Yes?"

But hadn't the old man just warned him against revealing such suspicions? "I think you're dangerous," Koji admitted.

"Dangerous." A pleased smile twitched the old man's lips. Then his face hardened. "Last night I asked you your clan name, but you did not answer. Have you learned manners yet?"

Koji's scalp felt hot with fear as he looked at the sword on the cave floor beside the old man. "Manners mean telling the truth," he whispered. "I have no clan name. My father is a farmer, and I am Kojiro, called Koji."

Dark Fire raised the sliding door of the bamboo cricket cage on his tray. Cooing to his pet, he slid out a leaf. He began to put a fresh one into the cage in its place, then noticed a slight blemish on it. He glanced over his shoulder at a guard kneeling behind him. "This leaf is unacceptable for my little dear one. Find another. Is Plum Blossom in camp now?"

"Yes."

"Bring her."

After the guard left, Dark Fire broke up twigs and dropped the pieces into the brazier. Then he folded his gnarled hands in his lap and rasped in a menacing tone, "Here is a riddle for you, farm boy. Who am I, and shall I let you live? Or . . . ?"

Koji realized that his jaw was hanging open and his eyes were as wide as the round eyes of a fish. "I hope you will." Gambling that flattery might help him, he said, "You're *samurai!*"

Another snort. "Are samurai outcasts who must hide in the forest like animals?"

"Well, no."

"You do have an idea what you have stumbled upon, but you are afraid to tell me." Dark Fire's eyes sharpened on Koji. "You are wise to fear me. Anytime we may be overheard, we call ourselves grass. Think of us that way and ask yourself no further questions about us." He reached behind, brought forward the crane cloth, and thrust it at Koji. "Why were you prowling through my forest, carrying the cloth of Udo-sama?"

When Koji shrank back in fright, the man dropped the cloth into his own lap. Delicately, he began turning his teacup around and around. Koji couldn't pull his eyes away. Each revolution felt like a rope twisting tighter and tighter around his own neck.

"The boy who captured you was on lookout duty. His orders were to kill anyone he found creeping around in my forest. Yet he didn't destroy you."

Koji's sweaty kimono collar stuck to his neck as the old man smoothed the crane cloth in his lap.

"This fabric is Udo-sama's. I conclude that you are from his castle. Logical?" He motioned to someone behind Koji, and a woman came forward. "Plum Blossom, you spend time at the castle and know all its residents. Is this a castle boy?"

A guard jerked Koji's head back for Plum Blossom to get a good look, and she leaned down and peered into his face. "No, he doesn't live at Crane Castle. I'm sure."

"Release him!" Dark Fire commanded. The guard let go of Koji's head and it bounced forward like a heavy gourd on a stem. Dark Fire took the fresh leaf another guard offered, examined it closely, then slid open the cricket cage door and put it inside.

Again Koji touched his forehead to the ground. "No, I'm not from the castle. Do you know the someru-ya? I—"

"The dye shop?" The old man gestured for the boy to show him his hand. When Koji did, the old man said thoughtfully, "Blue fingers. You work with dyes. Tanaka Shinzaemon has no children. . . . An apprentice?" He stared at Koji with strangely bright eyes. When Koji began to answer, he warned, "I have no patience with lies, farm boy."

Koji hardly knew how to explain. "I was hiding from Obaasan as she hung out the freshly dyed cloth and—"

"And you stole a piece?" A look of displeasure flickered over the man's face. "Are you that sort of boy?"

"No, I—"

"Pray tell," Dark Fire cut him off, "why did you want such a small piece of dyed cloth?"

Koji dug his nails into his palms. If he explained that Tanaka-sama had wrongfully given him the cloth, might he create trouble for the one person who had tried to give him a chance in life? But if he took the blame for having the cloth, what would this man do to him?

"You are quick-witted enough to know how to steal, but not how to cover your wrongdoing." Dark Fire's voice dripped acid.

"I didn't . . ."

Closing his eyes, Dark Fire turned his head away as if Koji were rancid meat. "I wish to tell you a story, and then I will ask you to do me a favor. It will be the first of many favors, I'm afraid, and you shall not refuse to do even one."

My story is about the world outside this forest," Dark Fire said. "The world of the samurai. Your world. It is inflexible and unalterable. A farmer is a farmer, and that changes only in the rarest of circumstances. And a samurai is a samurai. Unfairly, some people are even treated as outcasts. Everyone has his place, with its assigned behavior and rules. So your first lesson is this: There is a different way, and we live it here."

Dark Fire snapped his fingers. As if it were melting, the rock formation behind him in the gloom changed its contours. It seemed to come forward, turning into a shadow. Then Koji saw that it was not rock at all, but Spider, in a short hemp kimono. Smirking at Koji, he knelt beside Dark Fire.

"Just as in our world something may be rock one moment and a person the next, we in the forest live a life without clear lines, with everything blurred." Dark Fire raked his fingers through his sparse beard. "Four hundred years ago, your world was already as it is now. Rigid. Absolute. A samurai warrior called Kumagai-sama was fighting at the famous battle of Sumano-ura. He had an enemy in his grip and his sword raised to dispatch him to *gokuraku*.

"But the samurai code says that no warrior may take the life of one who is not at least his equal in rank. So he tore off his captive's helmet to find out whether or not he could honorably kill him. And what do you think he discovered?"

"Well . . . a warrior?"

"A boy still too young to grow a beard," Spider corrected in a smug tone. Obviously, he knew the story.

"He looked so much like Kumagai-sama's own son that Kumagai-sama said, 'Run away to safety, boy, because my army is close on my heels.'" Turning to the guard, Dark Fire added, "Serve these two tea."

While cups for Koji and Spider were placed on the tray between them, Dark Fire lovingly ran one finger along the side of his cricket cage. "Little dear one," he murmured, and the cricket hopped to his finger and began to chirp.

Though the tea tasted like boiled ashes, Koji drank it in gulps. He desperately wanted food but didn't dare ask for some.

"But the boy was from a samurai family, too," Dark Fire continued. "He reminded Kumagai-sama that according to the way of the warrior, the victor *must* slay the vanquished or he dishonors him. So he bared his young neck and begged to die."

"Didn't the boy love life?"

"He loved honor more," Spider said.

"It is the way of the samurai," Dark Fire agreed. "Though Kumagai-sama told him to run, the boy kept pleading to die. At last, Kumagai-sama heard the thunder of hooves. He cried out, 'If I don't slay this child now, someone less noble is sure to do it. And that will dishonor him. So Amida Buddha, receive his soul!' Then he slashed down his sword and killed the boy."

A shudder went through Koji.

"You don't find the story simple?"

"I wouldn't want to die if . . . But I'm not samurai."

"I, too, find the samurai's dilemma more complicated than he found it himself. Perhaps that's why I live here in the forest." Tapping one finger on his tray, the old man gazed off. "Had I been Kumagai-sama, do you know what I would have done?"

Spider answered, "Grandfather, he doesn't know anything."

"Grandson!" Dark Fire warned. Then he went on to Koji, "I would have tied and gagged that rascal and dragged him out of harm's way. When the battle was over, I would have sent him scampering home. You see, unlike the samurai, I do not find issues about honor and death easy. Honor is precious, but life is worth something, too. You look puzzled."

Koji summoned all his courage. "You say you

value life, yet last night you said you might . . . hurt me."

"You find me inconsistent." As before, the old man leaned down to cluck at his pet cricket. "But what is to you inconsistency is to me only ambiguity. You will find that many things in my world appear one way one moment and quite different the next. When my grandson found you invading my forest, he had no right to let you live."

Koji felt goose bumps. "Invading your forest? I was lost."

But Dark Fire sliced the air for silence. "Last night, I saw that you were a trespasser. But today I note that you are after all merely a child." He sat pulling on the sparse hairs of his beard. "When my grandson came upon you, he sized you up and let you live. Now I am curious to see whether he was foolish or wise." He motioned toward Spider, who tipped his head up arrogantly. "By sparing your life, my grandson linked his karma with yours. You have become his responsibility."

Spider's head came down as if he'd been hit. "I never meant to——"

"And water doesn't *mean* to reflect the moon, but it does. Now you are responsible for our farm boy." Dark Fire turned to Koji. "Model yourself after my grandson in every way. Learn what he knows." He snapped his fingers, and a guard appeared to escort Koji out of the cave.

"Please, I only want to go home," Koji begged. But even as he said it, a heaviness settled around his heart.

Now that he had disgraced his family, what would it feel like to be home?

"You have committed a grave offense. What would your master dye maker do if he found an enemy hiding among his dye pots?"

"He has no enemies," Koji said with a gulp.

Leaning forward, Dark Fire motioned Koji closer, then closer again until the boy was nose to nose with the old man. "But *I* have enemies," he whispered. "Shall you be my enemy, farm boy?"

"Never, never," Koji breathed, staggering back.

Dark Fire straightened up. "Just as I hoped." He smoothed the crane cloth with his clawlike hand. "Never become my enemy, little man, and you may go on living for a while longer."

Koji's neck felt painfully stiff as he placed his hands on his knees and bowed. It was an unbearable coincidence that, like the master dye maker, Dark Fire had called him "little man."

fter Dark Fire dismissed them to go eat breakfast, Koji and Spider sat before bowls of millet and chopped snake, set out on a stump. As fast as he could, Koji shoveled food into his mouth with chopsticks made out of twigs. Nearby, two women stood over a fire built outside the cooking cave. One roasted barley in a bamboo tube while the other ground bean paste in a mortar. Others sat eating in groups of two or three. Whenever someone went into the cooking cave for more food, they seemed to magically vanish behind the wisteria vines and melt into the cliff.

Falcon came strolling by, tossing a pickled plum from hand to hand. He'd already tried once to introduce himself to Koji. Now when he caught Koji's eye, he pitched the plum to him and walked over. "Introduce me to the village boy, Spider," he said as Koji devoured the plum.

"To this useless paddy frog? What for?"

"Then I'll introduce myself. I'm Falcon," the boy told Koji. "What village do you come from?"

"Falcon!" a man called, his hands on his hips.

Rolling his eyes, Falcon told Koji, "Somebody's always after me. So did you live in one of those warm farmhouses with the thatched roofs?"

Koji's jaw fell open. Warm? He remembered how the wind loved to whip through any chink in the house's construction, not to mention rattling the paper shoji screens on its way through.

The training master who'd called Falcon strode over and, with an indulgent smile, grabbed him by both shoulders and pulled him around. "Time for ground-hitting techniques."

With a grin and a shrug, Falcon sauntered off at his training master's side.

When Koji turned to Spider, he found the bigger boy gazing after Falcon disapprovingly. "'Warm house'! What kind of warrior is he to be longing for warmth? He's my best friend, but sometimes . . ." He glanced back at Koji and pinched his leg hard. "Your legs are as bony as a crane's." Koji flung his fist out to hit Spider, but the bigger boy caught his hand and pushed it away. "How can I make a fighter out of a bunch of bones?"

"A fighter? Me?"

"We're all fighters here. By the time you start going on missions, you'd better be able to fight, too."

Koji was dumbfounded. "Missions!" Then he turned away sullenly. "Leave me alone. I belong with my family."

Spider yanked him back. "From now on, we're your only family. That will never change."

"Don't other people here miss their families, too?"

"No, our families live here. Our whole clan is made of five families. No clan names, of course, but we know who we are! Although if someone lives outside of this camp or goes on a mission that lasts a long time, I suppose we miss them. But even then, we're not crying weaklings. He's my uncle," Spider added, pointing to the training master who had come for Falcon. "She's my grandfather's cousin," he added, pointing to a woman as she disappeared into the cooking cave.

"Who is Falcon related to?"

"You're nosy," Spider said coldly.

Startled and embarrassed, Koji changed the subject. "If you're all related, does that mean you all were born here?"

"Most of us. Which of you living soft lives in houses would willingly join us?"

"A farmer's life isn't soft."

"Soft!"

Koji flicked a glob of millet at Spider, and Spider's eyes turned hard, like rabbit pellets. "You're going to be trouble."

Trouble when? Koji wanted to ask, but he didn't dare. He shuddered at the implication that he had a future in this strange and threatening society.

Desperately, he looked around for an escape route. But he'd learned that a dozen boys Spider's age and older patrolled the forest, taking shifts at guarding the

camp for miles aro··
were not birds at a.
tem. More guards w

The guards were
like the one Spider ha(
few hours, they came o⌐
the cliff like spiders. Or th⌐
the woods, sparring. Their fi⌐
and cartwheels, somersaults ar.

Spider removed their empty
and sat thinking. "Your dye mak⌐
possessing two names as if he were⌐

"Master dye maker. And he ra.
than an ordinary craftsman—more ⌐
personal cloth artist. He taught me all at⌐
Koji added, surprised that he felt so prou⌐
shop where he had lived for such a short tir.
even created designs for the emperor."

"Was it the emperor who gave him the ⌐
bear a surname?"

"Yes."

"Hmm. But why would such a rich landowr⌐
snatch a useless farm boy from among peasants? It⌐
absurd!"

Perhaps not if Taro-the-Hero saved your life, Koji
thought bitterly. He muttered, "Tanaka-sama fell into
the river during a big storm and . . . Well, if a boy
saved your life, wouldn't you reward him?"

"Are you saying you saved Tanaka Shinzaemon's
life? Hard to picture you a hero," Spider sneered.

anted to change the subject from Taro's
How did that powder make you disappear in
ast night? And where did you go?"

nding he hadn't heard, Spider took their
to the cooking cave. He returned with a roll of
per and unrolled it to reveal a sketchy map of
walls and a few main corridors of some building.
moothed it out on the stump, set out a shaggy-
d writing brush, then dripped a little water into a
ll gourd. "Add details," he commanded, grinding
from an inkstick into the water. He stirred the ink
th his brush.

"I can't quite . . . recognize . . . ," Koji mumbled,
uzzled by the map and stalling.

"Surely you can tell me about Crane Castle?"

Koji glanced up, surprised. "Me?"

"When you've delivered dyed cloth for your high-
and-mighty master dye maker, you must have learned
the castle layout."

"Don't call him 'high and mighty.' He's a good man."

"A good landowner! Those two words are oppo-
sites."

"He was kind to me."

"Kindness to one person is nothing. Is a fisherman
good to the swimming fish because he leaves the riverbank for a few minutes? He's only going off to eat the
ones he's already caught." Spider tapped the map point-
edly.

"I've never been to the castle. Workmen deliver the
cloth."

Spider tipped up his chin. "Hard to believe!"

Koji stared at Spider. Last night he'd thought Spider was handsome. Now he reminded Koji of a narrow-faced rat with thick eyebrows.

Koji noticed Dark Fire nearby, leaning on two forked walking sticks. He was watching them. Frightened, Koji snatched up the brush and dipped it into the water in the gourd. As he held the brush over the map, a drop of ink dripped off and spread out on the paper.

"Look what you've done!" Spider cried.

Dark Fire limped closer. "Grandson, stop insisting that our farm boy knows the castle if he says he doesn't. You can take him there. Then—well. You know what I intend to learn."

Spider dipped his head in a bow. "Of course, Grandfather. I'd lost sight of the whole point."

Spider and Dark Fire both turned to gaze thoughtfully at Koji, and the boy's frantic glance darted from one face to the other. What were they talking about?

But neither explained. Dark Fire only said, "Grandson, let him rest for a few days and adjust to life here. Then go." He pulled on his long beard as his glance shifted to Koji. "Whether you have ever delivered cloth to Lord Udo is of no consequence. The point is that as apprentice to Tanaka Shinzaemon, the castle guards will admit you into the castle. Right? Once you are inside, surely you will do me the small favor of remaining alert. Later, tell my grandson what you saw. That's all I ask."

Dread washed over Koji as he watched Dark Fire hobble away. Go into Lord Udo's threatening castle full of samurai warriors?

An idea of how to escape suddenly occurred to him, and he scrambled to his feet. "I'm going to be sick! I'll be right back!" Holding one hand over his stomach and the other over his mouth, he tried to dash into the woods. But Spider lunged forward and snatched him back.

"Let go! I don't want to vomit here where you all live. I'll just run in among the trees." He tried to squirm out of Spider's grip. "Only for a moment!"

"No! Vomit right here," Spider challenged, shaking him hard, like a dog with a rat.

When Koji realized that his trick hadn't worked, his chin sank onto his chest.

"I knew you were lying, you faker. You're full of tricks, but they're all childish. You'll never escape from me." Spider tossed his head back. "If you knew about some of the missions I've been on . . . When I fight, I leap, I flip, I fly."

Koji's mouth twitched in disgust. "Who *are* you people?" he asked, as he had before. "You're not . . ." But he didn't even dare say that dangerous word—ninja.

"Don't you listen? Grandfather and I have both told you we're grass." Spider shuffled his foot through the turf. "We're grass because we're invisible. You're grass, too, but because Udo-sama grinds you under his heel."

Koji stared blankly at the grass and remembered that Dark Fire had told him the same thing.

"You have bruises there," Spider added in a pleased tone, and Koji touched his neck. Spider flexed his hands proudly. "I made them capturing you."

"Is everyone here as cruel as you?" Koji growled.

"Cruel, us? Ha! Is your world all loving kindness? What if Udo-sama passed by and you didn't scramble to your knees?"

Koji looked away uncomfortably.

"He would slice off your head. We both know he would. With those two long swords that he can carry because he is samurai—and that you can't carry, because you're not. And if you saw his blade swinging through the air to cut you in two, you would pull out your own sword and . . ."

"You know a poor farmer wouldn't stand a chance against a samurai's sword."

"Oho!" Spider crowed. "Then I suppose you would defend yourself with something like this." He snatched up a weak branch and danced around, brandishing it.

He broke it in two to show how flimsy it was, then tossed down the pieces. "Later—you would be dead by then—the other farm boys might invent a better weapon than a branch." He strode to a pile of weapons near the base of a pine and pulled out a small sickle. Attached to it was a long cord, weighted at the end. "This is a *mamukigama*," he said. "You tie a live snake onto the cord and throw it at your victim. He's so busy coping with the snake that you can easily attack him with the blade. I bet the sickle you used in farming had a blade like this."

"Yes, it did," Koji said, eyeing it. "What are you saying?"

"That our ancestors were peasant farmers, like you. We're on the same side. We both hate Lord Udo. But while you'll be a timid paddy frog all your life, we're working to destroy Udo-sama. We do it with stealth, hiding even behind grass. Close your eyes."

Koji did, and soon Spider said, "Now open."

When he opened his eyes, Spider was gone. "Find me," came his voice.

"I can't," Koji said after a moment of looking around.

"What about the tree?"

Puzzled, Koji peered at the chestnut tree before him. Spider's voice did seem to come from behind it. But there was a jog in the trunk a few feet up, as if when it was young the tree had been cut to a high stump, then had continued growing from it at an odd angle. It wasn't possible, Koji thought, for Spider to be hiding behind a trunk shaped like that.

"Come around," Spider called.

Koji looked behind the tree. He was astonished to find Spider hiding there. His body was molded exactly to the trunk's peculiar shape. Obviously, Spider had dislocated his shoulder to follow the gnarled trunk. His hip was out of its joint, too, and dropped slightly to hide behind the high stump.

When Spider shifted, his body dissolved from the

bizarre configuration into its usual form. His face showed pain as he pressed his shoulder, then his hip against the tree to replace the bones in their joints. "I'm extraordinary," he declared with a pompous wave of his hand. "That's why I'm called Spider."

"Everyone hates spiders. Besides, they're unlucky."

Spider swatted Koji. "I'm called Spider because I climb walls like one. And I fight as if I have eight arms and legs."

"I bet whoever nicknamed you Spider wanted to squash you."

Spider set his jaw as if to proclaim that he was too mature to let Koji's childish jabbering annoy him. "Remember, I was supposed to kill you." He shoved Koji good-naturedly. "Your first mission, in just a few days! Are you excited?"

"What does your grandfather want me to notice in the castle?" Koji asked nervously.

"For one thing, which floors squeak more than others."

"Why would any floors squeak?"

"Don't ask questions! Just do as I say! And notice where stairways are, also any large bells, jars set out as ornaments . . . big ones, I mean. Man-sized. Places where people could hide, back entrances, things like that."

"Why do you want to know those things? And if you're going to the castle with me, why don't *you* notice them?"

"My noticing isn't the point. And remember, I'll be grass."

"You'll be hidden?"

"Invisible. If someone catches you creeping around in the wrong part of the castle, say you're lost and act scared."

"I will be scared."

"Just remember that even if you don't see me, I'm nearby."

"To protect me?"

But Spider didn't answer. "Look, I know last night was frightening for you, and today has been hard. I'll give you five days to rest and adjust. Then we go on the mission to Crane Castle."

uring the days before Koji's mission, fear and worry and boredom and misery all wrapped themselves up together and lodged in his gut. Sometimes Spider trained him in basic sparring techniques. More often, Spider was busy with his own training, and Koji sat alone, watching the three twelve- and thirteen-year-olds—Sky, Minnow, and Spider's cousin, Raven Wing—train.

"Koji, come help," Sky called to him one day when it was their turn to work with the snakes and wood frogs raised to be used on missions. Koji hurried to join Sky and the two girls. The village rice paddies were full of frogs, and he felt proud that he handled these wood frogs confidently. But when Minnow offered him what looked like a poisonous bamboo snake, he instinctively shrank away from it.

"Look, he's scared!" Raven Wing sneered.

Koji knew he'd humiliated himself and, clenching his jaw, forced himself to reach toward the snake. But Minnow was already leaning down to put the snake back into its cage. Raven Wing swept a bouquet from where she'd held it tucked under her sash. She drew a hidden dagger from it, and when she jabbed it at Koji, he recoiled again.

"Don't mind her—she treats Minnow and me that way, too," Sky told Koji after Raven Wing had started away, laughing. But the damage was done, and they didn't invite Koji over again.

Left alone, Koji would wander through those caves that were used as small factories. People made weapons from farm implements in one cave, sewed disguises in a second, and raised the snakes and frogs in a third.

For training purposes, thorny vines stretched at all angles in some of the black passages between caves. Koji liked to crawl through them in deep darkness, trying to avoid the obstacle course. But once, he cut his leg so badly that he needed to visit the cave of Minnow's great-aunt, mystical Clear Mist, with her magical powders and herbs. Chanting a spell, she used her finger to stroke *sha,* the character for healing, over his wound. Then she bandaged it over an onion salve.

When Dark Fire saw the injury, he warned Koji not to do any more training until he was properly taught how. After that, Koji was more bored than ever. Usually, no one seemed to pay attention to him as he explored the camp. But whenever he strayed near the forest, a guard was sure to leap down from a tree and push him back toward the center of the training camp.

He was grateful when darkness dropped over the mountain each evening, grateful that he'd lived through one more of the five days he must pass in this awful glade, grateful even though his nights alone under guard in the drafty "prison cave" were even more miserable than his days.

He couldn't wait until Spider took him into the valley. What fools these people were, planning to send him to Crane Castle! He knew he could never find his way down the densely wooded mountain. But once they delivered him into his own world in the valley, he felt sure he could escape. *And my family* does *want me back,* he told himself with his jaw clenched. He would not let himself even wonder about the other horrible possibility.

At twilight on the fifth day, Koji felt flooded with joy. Finally, he and Spider were about to set off down the sheer mountain. He couldn't wait to clear things up with Taro, to explain to Mama and Papa that the mess he'd made of things at the someru-ya had been pure accident, to tell them all that he hadn't meant to run away from them, as they must think.

And to hear them answer, smiling, that they were pleased with him . . . proud! Proud of so many things about him . . . What had he been wondering? Whether they thought he'd shamed them? *Impossible, dear firstborn son of ours.*

Perhaps Papa would even draw him aside and

whisper, "Never let Taro know, but we've always loved you best."

No clear path led down the craggy mountain from the secret camp. But neither did Spider and Koji break underbrush as they moved through the forest at sunset. Instead, Spider showed Koji how to slither through openings between bushes and trees, leaving the foliage untouched. When they neared the bottom of the mountain and Koji started recognizing where he was, Spider whipped out a cloth, blindfolded Koji, and dragged him along.

When Spider untied the blindfold, they were in a bamboo forest beside the darkening road from Kurikawa to Udo-sama's castle. In nearby paddies, rice shoots stood up out of the water and swayed in the breeze. A heron alighted in one of them.

It was all so familiar and beloved to Koji.

"It's time for you to head to the castle, paddy frog. Remember, you must tell us all that you see, so pay attention to everything." Spider paused, then added, "Now I'll become grass."

"You mean you're leaving already?" Koji couldn't believe his good luck. He reached back and patted the crane cloth stuck under his sash to be sure it was still there. If Spider was fool enough to abandon him here on the road he knew so well, he could easily escape.

"Just because you don't see me, don't think I'm gone," Spider warned as if he were reading Koji's mind. "My hiding skills are remarkable. The training masters praise me so often they bore me." He gave Koji a push toward the road. "You won't see me again until you're back here. But I will be with you. Remember, go straight to the castle. Hide, though, don't go along the road where you might be seen. No village. No dye shop. No family. No friends."

"How can you . . ."

"How is none of your business! And if you feel a drop of water on your cheek or see a pebble thrown—anything like that—I'm signaling you."

"How long do I have to stay in the castle?" Koji asked, gazing in its direction. When Spider didn't answer, Koji glanced around. But Spider was gone.

This was Koji's world, not Spider's, and he felt confident. The worst five days of his life were finished, and surely something would happen to free him before he reached the castle.

For good luck, Koji pulled the Jizo out of the front pocket of his kimono. Except for one rough spot on Jizo's robe, it was smooth, even polished, first from Papa's careful work, then from the family's hands rubbing it over the years. It puzzled Koji that Papa had been careless in one and only one spot, but that was the spot Koji's thumb always found. Sometimes that one sloppy patch on the precisely carved statue felt like all that connected Koji, not Taro, to Papa.

As he passed the rice paddies, he slowed down to listen to the croaking frogs. Their serenade reminded him of hot evenings when he had caught fireflies with Taro. When the fields were flooded like this, they often "accidentally" pushed each other down between the rows of tender plants. The water was always so cool.

Koji continued plodding along, reluctantly staying back from the road, hidden behind trees and bushes, as Spider had commanded. He went by the head of one of Udo-sama's enemies, posted on a stake. It had been rotting there for weeks, and Koji licked his finger and wet his eyebrows. Looking the other way with his eyes squeezed shut, he ran past the decaying head as fast as he could.

Crane Castle appeared around the next bend in the road. Koji dreaded continuing toward the frightening place. Its whitewashed walls rose up in a sloping foundation and stood out brightly against the evening sky. It was called Crane Castle because the white walls with scarlet roof tiles were like a white crane with red on its head. Two tiger-headed bronze fish, one at either end of the upturned tile roof, raised their arched tails skyward to ward off fire.

The circle of shops and warriors' homes around Crane Castle looked busy with important strangers. To Koji, every one of them was threatening. Lights from oil lamps and torches danced along the streets. The river was a black stripe. Its ripples shone like a gigantic snake's moving back.

Koji glanced around for Spider, then slipped past the *torii* gate and down the path surrounded by dense *sakaki* evergreens to the wooden temple. Dramatically, he wiped his brow to notify Spider, wherever he was, that he was only stopping because he was hot and tired.

As the monks began chanting prayers inside, he sat down on the edge of the well. He laid his hand on the well's mossy wooden edging and let the mud squish up through his straw sandals and between his toes. His eyes fluttered shut. He prayed to the temple's *kami-sama. Please don't make me go to that castle!*

Something clattered. He looked up, startled. Not three feet away, the well's squeaky handle revolved recklessly. The bucket was rolling down. Loudly, it splashed into the water below.

The taut rope trembled. Was this one of Spider's signals? Outrage rose up inside Koji. Couldn't he rest for a moment?

With his jaw set in anger, Koji closed his eyes again. But this time he heard a grating sound nearby. He opened his eyes to find that the bucket had been cut loose, and a short piece of rope dangled free. It warned Koji as clearly as if Spider had spoken: I held my knife near your neck. Next time I will cut *you.*

Koji knew he had no choice and stood up. He slapped the dust off his kimono, then started tramping toward the castle. Soon he was in the busy castle town, passing shops and the public bathhouse. People streamed by him, even now in the evening. Vegetable and tofu sellers called out their wares while baskets swung from yokes on their shoulders. There were shaven-headed monks in hemp robes and a night watchman setting out with his lantern and noisy wooden clappers.

He passed the timbered homes of lower- and then

higher-ranking samurai warriors, and then the earthen wall that marked the start of the castle grounds. Horsemen sat astride lacquered saddles powdered with gold dust. Little samurai boys strutted proudly, always keeping their hands on the wooden swords at their hips. In high watchtowers, warriors in leather armor and crested helmets scanned the countryside. More were stationed at intervals around the outer walls. Some held up lanterns, their paper panes marked with the Udo crest. Others were shadowy forms in the dim light.

Koji heard Spider's sharp hototogisu call and looked around. These outer grounds were all long shadows. He suddenly realized it was no accident that they'd come to the castle in the evening. Surely, Spider could hide more easily now than during the day.

The bird call again. As Koji trudged onto the drawbridge over the moat, he caught up with a young woman. She wore a simple springtime kimono and the white rice-flour face powder of court ladies. Her eyebrows were shaved, and others were drawn in, higher. Idly moving a painted fan as she walked, she looked up and around when she heard the hototogisu. When she caught Koji's eye, she smiled.

He smiled back as he passed her, crossing the drawbridge toward the *tenshu*'s riveted gate. Koji was afraid of its guard, who looked formidable in his armor and conical iron hat. The boy stalled by leaning over the drawbridge railing and looking at the lotus leaves that floated on the moat's surface.

As he gazed down, a spray of pebbles hit the clear water. Moonlit drops flew up like crystals while the pebbles sank into the murk. *Another warning from Spider,* Koji realized unhappily, and he approached the nearby guard. "I'm the apprentice to Tanaka Shinzaemon," he murmured, bowing low.

"So?"

"Well, I brought this piece of cloth," he began, then realized he was backing away in fear. *Spider is right,* he thought with dismay, *I am nothing but a timid paddy frog.* He took a deep breath, planted his feet firmly, then looked the guard in the eye. "A piece of cloth," he repeated loudly, and held it out to him.

Thrusting his lantern close, the guard sneered. He was missing his front teeth. "You must be not only new at the someru-ya but a fool, too. Do you think Udo-sama wants his cloth delivered in single scraps?" He shoved Koji. "Be gone!"

Koji stumbled back and fell in an undignified sprawl.

oji started to get up. Then, as people streamed past him in and out of the castle, he had an idea. *If I pester the guard a second time, won't he want to drive me away?* He clamped his jaw hard, stood, and stepped up to the guard. *Annoy him as much as you can,* he told himself. *Whine!*

Pretending to pout, he held out the cloth again. Even before he spoke, the guard shoved him away. This time Koji made a point of falling hard. He waved his small piece of cloth at the guard, thinking, *See how irritating I am? Don't just knock me down. Drive me far away!*

But the guard only turned his back on Koji. Four carriers of a lacquer-and-brass sedan chair glanced down at him as they marched by and started laughing. Inside the sedan chair, someone was playing a flute. The melody had a high little trill, and Koji felt as if even the tune were mocking him. But he didn't care. If shame could keep him out of Crane Castle, then he longed to be shamed.

"Guard, please!" he cried, holding the cloth up high.

As if in response to the commotion outside, the flute music inside the sedan chair stopped. The reed window was lowered and a nobleman's face appeared. His long forelock told Koji he wasn't much older than Spider.

The young man reached through the window and tapped his fan on the outside of the sedan chair. At the signal, the carriers put it down. "Hey, little pest!" the young man called to Koji. "What's this disruption all about?"

Something about the young nobleman was even more frightening than the guard, and Koji scrambled to his feet. Bowing, he held out the fabric respectfully in both trembling hands. "I brought cloth to Lord Udo." He looked up at the young man from under his brows, saw only as high as his sneering mouth, and backed away. "But I've changed my mind."

"Oh, is that so?" The young man stepped out of the sedan chair and looked Koji up and down. He wore an elaborate *kamishimo*: starched trousers, or *hakama,* and the winged jacket of a samurai. A flute was tucked into his sash. "Guard! Don't you realize that this important personage must see Lord Udo?"

Sarcastic meanness had slithered between his words. Koji pulled up his shoulders as if he could hide his head like a turtle.

But the guard only bowed. "As you wish, my lord."

The young man glanced around at Koji. "Must you keep goggling at me?" He motioned for his carriers to take the sedan chair onward without him. Then he stepped so near Koji that the boy could smell the camellia flower oil that slicked down the young man's topknot. "Come with me!" he commanded. As he strode along, his geta made impressive *tonk tonk tonk*ing sounds on the drawbridge. Koji's straw sandals only shushed as he scurried to keep up.

They passed through several gates and crossed the castle's inner yard, dotted with greenery and stone lanterns. Koji had never seen such an impressive and beautiful garden and gulped as he stared. "Please, I don't want to see Udo-sama," he squeaked as he clutched his scrap of cloth with white-knuckled hands.

"I'm sure you don't, but you're going to," the young man said, clamping a hand on Koji's shoulder.

Remembering how Taro had changed after he thought Koji was teasing about failing at the someru-ya, he said, "It was only a joke." He wriggled to get free. "Please let me go."

But the young man tightened his clutch and pushed Koji forward. "Dangerous to joke with samurai . . . If my father laughs hard enough, perhaps he'll put your head up on a stake. We can, you know. We samurai can cut you down just for looking at us."

"Your father?" Koji was really frightened now.

"That's right," the young man said, tossing his head just like Spider. "My father is Lord Udo."

Then they were inside the castle itself. Young Lord Udo sauntered down corridors alive with murals of dragons and tigers playing among bamboo. He appeared to be comfortable in the stunning and luxurious surroundings. Beside him, though, Koji stumbled along feeling clumsy and unsophisticated. He tried to pull out of young Lord Udo's grasp. But it was impossible.

In one wooden corridor, the floor squeaked underfoot. It was the feature Spider had told Koji to focus on. He glanced up at the young man and parted his lips to ask about it. But young Udo-sama's haughty expression silenced him.

"Here we are." The young man stopped before a flimsy door of paper in a wood frame. Beside it stood a guard in horizontally striped breeches and a flowered jacket. Ignoring him, young Udo-sama touched the door to open it.

The guard held out his hand to stop them. "With respect . . ."

The young man flashed him a defiant glance. "You dare question me?" he asked dangerously, and the guard stepped back. The young man slid open the paper door just wide enough to slip through. But instead of stepping inside himself, he thrust Koji through the doorway and yanked the door shut.

Propelled by the shove, Koji stumbled into a big reception room and stared with his mouth hanging open. Most of the space was filled by a raised platform carpeted with tatami mats. Behind it hung a scroll painting on silk of foggy mountains. The pillars set around the room were trimmed with gold leaf. Sticks of incense stood in jars of ashes, scenting the air.

Two samurai knelt on the platform, talking. Each of their jackets was stamped with a family crest: Udo-sama's, a crane, and his guest's, an open umbrella. Behind them, a dozen swords were displayed on a rack. Next to it, armor hung on a stand.

Koji pressed his back against the door. He groped behind for the wood slat to slide the door open. But when he found it and pushed, it wouldn't budge. Lord Udo's son had to be holding the door shut from the other side.

Koji thought of breaking right through the paper wall to escape. But fear paralyzed him. He prayed to Amida Buddha, *Please get me out of here. Please. Please!*

"Who are you?" rumbled Lord Udo. In the flickering light of a candle on a tall stand, his angry face looked like a tengu's. "How dare you enter this room? Guard!"

The samurai with Lord Udo had knobby shoulders and big horsey teeth that he tried to hide behind tight lips. His face was flat. "Calm down, Udo-san. You saw what happened. The arm that pushed him in here wore pale blue. Your son?"

"Yes, I suppose it was Norimaru," Lord Udo grumbled.

So that's his name, Koji thought. He imagined how foolish he must have looked as he groveled before the guard on the drawbridge. *Norimaru could have come to my aid as I sprawled there looking so helpless,* he thought. *But he didn't, he made things worse.* Koji's face throbbed with humiliation. He knew he would never forget that scornful flute melody.

"Then for once Norimaru's foolish teasing is well timed," the visitor said. "This boy has arrived at the perfect moment. Let him settle the question." He motioned Koji forward.

Not budging, Koji stuffed the crane cloth under the back of his sash. He was sure it would create trouble for him.

The visitor motioned Koji forward again. "Don't be afraid."

From the conversation, Koji guessed that this visitor was superior even to Lord Udo. He forced himself to go and kneel before the men.

A long wood-and-metal object lay on the tatami mat in front of them. The flat-faced samurai picked it up and handed it to Koji. The boy held his breath as he took it. The thing looked menacing, with a thin metal tube that ran two-thirds of its length. A rounded wooden piece angled down from one end in a sort of handle. Between the tube and wooden portions, a metal mechanism looked as if it must click back and forth.

"Who are you?" Lord Udo barked again.

Koji leaned forward to touch the floor with his forehead. But before he could answer, the flat-faced samurai spoke.

"If you desist from grilling him for a moment, perhaps he can help us." Turning back to Koji, he added, "We were having a disagreement, boy, before you were, shall we say, ushered in here." He motioned toward the metal-and-wood thing Koji held. "Do you know what that is?"

"No, samurai-sama."

"Can you guess?"

Koji shifted it to get a better look. "Is it . . . a weapon?"

"Clever boy! Have you ever seen such a weapon before?"

"I've seen swords, spears, lances. Things like that."

"Of course. Those are the weapons we've always used here in Japan. This one is something new. It's foreign. Did you know there are other places in the world besides Japan?"

"Yes, samurai-sama. China and Korea."

"There are more places than that. This thing is from Portugal, where the people are big, with brown faces and sharp noses. Hardly like people at all. That weapon you're holding is called a 'musket.' Lord Udo and I want to make many like it for our soldiers. But parts of it aren't easy to copy. Can you guess how the weapon works?"

"I suppose you point it, this way."

"Again you prove your intelligence! But hold it higher. By your face. You look down the tube at what you're shooting. That way, you can aim straighter."

Koji raised the musket to his eye and pointed it at a lacquer-and-mother-of-pearl vase.

"If you'd like to try it, you may pull back on that hook."

Koji slid his finger into the space in front of the trigger. When he squeezed, the attached hammer clicked forward.

"It isn't loaded now," the visitor said. "But when it is, something comes out of the end of that long tube."

Koji turned it to look down the barrel. "A dart?"

"More like a firecracker." The flat-faced samurai held his hand out to take the musket back.

"Why show such a thing to a peasant?" Lord Udo growled.

"To prove the point I was making before he came in. You're wrong when you say that only horsemen and generals should have muskets. If a mere boy can aim and pull the trigger, so can a foot soldier." Smiling broadly, the samurai folded his hands. "You and I have taught Lord Udo something today, haven't we, boy? Samurai don't have a corner on intelligence."

Koji was sure Lord Udo would not welcome learning a lesson from him. "May I go, samurai-sama?"

Someone slid open the door. It was the same young woman who had crossed the drawbridge with Koji and smiled at him after hearing the hototogisu . . . Spider. After kneeling to close the door, she stood up and took tiny, sliding steps as she carried a tea tray to the men.

"Boy, do you—" the visitor began.

"Get him out of here!" Udo-sama roared at the woman. She froze, holding the tray high over her head so that her breath wouldn't graze the food and drink. "Take him to . . . Do you work here, boy?" Lord Udo demanded.

The woman tilted her head to acknowledge Koji. "Don't you work in the stables?" she asked him gently, cutting off his answer. "Lord Udo, I will see that he gets there."

"Boy, next time you bother me—"

"I'll make sure he is not naughty again," the young woman promised. She scurried to set the tray down before the men, and soon she was escorting Koji through the castle. She smelled of cloves.

Koji hurried along at the young woman's side. "I saw you on the drawbridge," he said.

"Yes. That guard is more bad tempered than a hungry tiger. Don't mind him. You did nothing wrong."

"Thank you!" Koji cried. Then he added cautiously, "Can you direct me out of the castle instead of to the stables? I don't know my way out from this part of the castle."

"You don't know your way out from any part of the castle," she murmured, staring ahead. "You can stop pretending. I know you don't work in the stables or anywhere else in Crane Castle."

Koji was too shocked to answer.

She removed the fan from the broad obi folded behind her as if a big butterfly had landed on the small of her back. Hiding her mouth with the fan, she murmured, "I am O Kei, lady in waiting to Udo-san's daughter. Udo-san may not know everyone who works in the castle, but I do. And you are not one of them."

"You protected me in there."

She inclined her head graciously. "Certainly. I do not normally serve Lord Udo his tea. But I saw the altercation between you and the guard, and once Norimaru took an interest in you, I knew you might need my help."

"Norimaru pushed me into the reception room."

"Yes, so I took the tray from the serving woman and found a way to escort you out."

"I never saw you nearby at all," Koji said in amazement. When she didn't answer, he gave her a quick bow as he walked. "Thank you!"

"And . . . turn here . . . then you encountered yet another predicament. One before Udo-san."

"Yes, I—"

She held up a delicate hand. "You needn't explain yourself," she said quietly. "I know young Udo Norimaru. On the one hand, he plays that flute in tones you'd think could only come from Amida Buddha himself. When he strolls through the castle gardens, playing in the evening, his father leaves whatever he's doing to come listen. But in every other way, that young man is a tengu in samurai's clothes."

Koji stopped listening as he remembered again the guard knocking him down on the drawbridge and relived hearing the sneers and laughter all around him.

". . . there, in the northern corridor," he realized O Kei was saying as she gestured with her fan.

"Huh?" Koji asked. He stopped walking, then realized he'd been abruptly impolite and bowed, blushing.

Covering her mouth with her hand, O Kei giggled quietly. "Your manners remind me of my small brother," she said, then added almost under her breath, "I was pointing out that in that hallway slender threads cross from side to side. They were strung there only yesterday."

Koji glanced at her. What a strange thing to say. But her odd comment did remind him that this whole time he should have been paying close attention to the castle's details. Especially which floors squeaked more than others. If he could supply the single piece of information Spider wanted most of all, he thought the older boy might be satisfied with his efforts.

"O Kei-sama," he said, hoping he sounded innocent, "the corridor outside the reception room where I saw Udo-sama . . . I've never heard floorboards so squeaky!"

Again O Kei used her fan to hide her mouth. "Yes, that hallway floor . . . that third right turn off the main corridor . . . the one with all the latticework . . . is intentionally squeaky."

She gave him a sharp, meaningful glance, but Koji didn't understand. "Intentionally squeaky?"

"The squeaking serves the same purpose as the threads." When he still didn't comprehend, she added, "Those living in castles must be careful."

"I know nothing about life in castles. I'm only a farm . . ." Then, thinking of the crane cloth still hidden in the folds of his sash, he finished, ". . . a dye maker's apprentice."

"I told you not to pretend with me. Like the threads, the squeaky 'nightingale floor' is a trap."

"A trap for?"

She looked baffled. *"Shinobi,"* she said. When Koji didn't react, she added, "You do not know this word, you who are obviously here to . . . *Rappa,* then?" Again she glanced at him questioningly, but again Koji drew a blank. "Ninja?"

Koji caught his breath. Ninja.

"Revolting, those creatures," she said distantly. "They don't fight openly like samurai. Instead, they creep in over back walls, hide in bells, behind gongs, even over ceilings and under floors. They are spies without honor."

Fear crept up on him like ants on the march. *My suspicions were right,* he thought. *Where is Ninja Spider? Is he hiding overhead? Is he crouched under the floor, itching to cut my throat for speaking on such a topic?*

Accidentally, he stumbled against O Kei. When she didn't push him away, he felt an impulse to spill his whole story about getting lost in the fog and the ninja camp. *I could beg her to protect me,* he thought, *and to take me home to Kurikawa.*

He opened his mouth to speak, but suddenly O Kei jerked him around by the shoulder. She pushed him through a door, then shut it behind them. They

stood at the top of a staircase. Below, it was as black as the inside of a cauldron.

"Hurry! Go down!" She nudged him and he descended, groping along the stone wall. At the bottom, O Kei pulled him around again.

Although she stood before him, it was too dark for Koji to see her. "Where—where are we?" he stammered.

"This is a secrecy room. Unlike the paper-walled rooms upstairs, this one is lined with stone. No one can hear us here. Not even Spider."

Koji felt as if she'd flung snow in his face. "You know about Spider?"

"I heard his bird call. He's my second cousin."

"I hate Spider. He captured me. And he's one of those ninja. Please . . ."

She laid her delicate hand on his shoulder, and he threw his arms around her as if he were drowning.

"Stop! Stop! I can't breathe!" she cried softly.

"Help me!" But the hug embarrassed him, too, and he let go.

"I can guess your story. Lost in the forest? But I can't help you. A fish on the cutting board must settle for being thrown into a bucket of water. If you want to go on living, loyalty to us is your only hope."

Bleakly, he stared into the darkness. "Us?"

"We are grass. Now that you've annoyed Udo-sama, you should get out of the castle quickly. I brought you into this secrecy room to tell you how. Go through the arch on the left, then through the women's quarters. Act calm but confused about where you are. You're so young, the ladies will hardly notice you. They'll only direct you out and won't call the guard."

"Please, I . . ."

"From the women's quarters, walk straight ahead to the gate. Don't worry about finding Spider. He'll find you. Now go back up. When I signal you, walk away from me. And get out."

He took one step up the stairs, then looked over his shoulder, although in the dark he couldn't even see O Kei's shape. "Please help me," he begged one last time. Panic cracked his voice. But O Kei only gave him another little push.

At the top of the stairs, she reached around him, slid open the shoji screen, and shoved him out. He stood with his head bowed in defeat until she pinched his arm. Then he stumbled forward. They walked together for a while before she looked sidelong at him and gave him the slightest of nods. She turned down another corridor, leaving him alone.

Kei had told him to stay calm. But he couldn't help himself—he ran. He dashed headlong, straight ahead, then through the left arch. He blundered into the women's quarters. Ladies jumped back from him. Giggling, a girl Koji's age snatched at him as he ran. He skidded on a kimono that lay on the floor and flung both arms out to catch himself. But as he fell, he knocked a makeup box off a dressing table. *Crash!* Down with the box came bamboo combs, shells filled with feather brushes and rouge. Lavender scent blossomed in the air.

But as the makeup box broke, he picked himself up and sprinted on. His heart thumped in his ears: *Escape! Escape!*

In a flash, he was beyond the havoc and in the serene inner courtyard, dotted with mossy gardens. Here and there, lanterns cast pools of light into the darkness. Staggering, he grabbed hold of a bush. Thrushes, settled for the night, flew up from it. As he stood gulping for air, a guard strolled by, looking him over.

"Calm down, boy."

Koji made his way through the gate between the inner and outer courtyards. He snatched a handful of firecrackers from a basket, probably left over from the rice-planting celebrations. He stuffed them into the front of his kimono.

Afraid Spider would catch him if he passed through the main gate as O Kei had suggested, he jogged along the outer wall instead. He hid in shadows and behind foliage until he came to a bamboo tree. He looked around wildly to make sure Spider was not there, then up at the wall. He longed to escape over it, but it was high and sheer. Although . . .

He stuck his sandals under his sash and, with flaring hope, climbed the bamboo. A guard came patrolling, but it was dusk and he didn't seem to notice the thick place on the bamboo trunk where Koji was frozen in place.

Fear dried out his mouth as he began to inch his way up again. Soon he was level with the top of the wall. The breeze cooled his face. The distant rice paddies shone in the moonlight. Freedom.

"Hey!" Sudden scurrying below. "You, boy, up there!"

He pushed himself higher as the guard below shook the tree.

"Get down here, you scamp!"

Under Koji's weight, the tree dipped toward the wall.

"There's a brat up this tree! Come help me!"

Koji's heart drummed as he moved that last little bit. Finally, the pliant tree drooped far enough to dangle him over the wall. He sprang out into the air. As he fell, the garden flashed by with more guards running toward him.

He lay panting on the safe side of the wall. On the other side, guards were still shouting.

Koji clambered to his feet. He didn't know whether to strike out across the paddies or follow the shorter route home by road. Spider didn't know which village he came from, so Koji gambled that he would be as safe on the road to Kurikawa as anywhere else. He dashed down the dark, empty road and over the arched bridge crossing the river. His side spasmed from running so hard. He clutched it, gulping, and stumbled off again.

If I reach that cherry tree, he told himself, *I will get home without Spider catching me.* Once the cherry tree was over his shoulder he told himself, *If I make it to that broken old ox cart, I'm definitely safe.* He tweaked the lapel of his kimono and peeked in at the firecrackers. Wait until Taro saw them!

As he reached the cart, someone called him from behind. "Help an old man," came the weak voice.

When Koji didn't respond, the voice came again: "Don't you respect your elders?"

Warily, Koji looked back. A *komuso* monk, presumably from the nearby monastery in the mountains, hobbled on a walking stick. Like any komuso, he wore a basket hat. Except for the eye holes, it covered his whole head. *It's Spider,* Koji thought.

But as if the old man had read his mind, he swept the basket hat off his head and revealed his face. Despite the dim light, Koji saw that he had long gray hair, all matted. One eyeball was cloudy, like a silver-gray stone.

Still looking over his shoulder, Koji went on taking hesitant steps forward. The poor old man. "What can I do, Grandfather?"

The old man angled his head to look at Koji with his one seeing eye. "It's hard enough walking in the dark evening, and now a pebble is caught in my sandal," he complained. "Come close, boy. Let me lean on you while I adjust it."

Koji turned back and held out his hand. The old man reached toward him but wobbled. "Come closer," he said, and Koji fitted himself under the old man's shoulder. He was barely in place before the old man's arm shot around him. It was as strong as a chain. Koji knew that grip and squeezed his eyes shut in blank despair. But he didn't try to pull away. He was beaten.

Spider gripped Koji so tightly that his ribs seemed to crush his heart. Then the bigger boy pushed his face close. "You think you can run away?" he whispered fiercely. "I have disguises like this hidden everywhere. I can become anyone. Fast. Don't ever try to escape from me again." He touched his mock-blind eye with his forefinger and detached something from his eyeball. Koji barely had a chance to see that the thing was a fish scale before Spider slapped the basket hat down over Koji's head and shoved him forward.

Koji plodded away from Kurikawa. With the eye slits turned to one side, all he could see was the inside of the basket hat. But he didn't care.

"Quit dragging your feet," Spider spat, but Koji dawdled more than before. "Look at me," Spider commanded. Koji shook his head to adjust the basket hat's eye slits, and Spider flashed his open hand into Koji's view. Spider held one of the steel stars he had threatened Koji with in the forest. "If you don't walk faster, I'll cut you."

Like bellows giving up air, all the fight went out of Koji. He trudged along with his head down in defeat.

After a while, Spider stretched his arms. "We're alone and safe and Kurikawa is out of sight," he announced brightly.

Koji was amazed. "You know I'm from Kurikawa?"

"That night when you were lost, you told the trees you were from Kurikawa, remember?"

Koji did recall speaking out loud when he'd been lost. The sound of a voice, even his own, had soothed him a little. But if he'd known what talking to himself would lead to . . . !

As Spider pulled the basket hat off Koji, the younger boy held up pleading hands. "Please! Kurikawa is home!"

"Good point." Spider grabbed him by the arm. Still

wearing the disguise, he strode fast and pulled Koji along behind. "Someone might come along who knows you. . . . So I guess you met Jade Bat? At the castle, they call her O Kei," he added.

Something reckless, like a trapped hummingbird, flapped wildly in Koji's heart. "You people are those ninja!"

"Shh! You can say that word in the camp and in private. But don't say it out in the open. We are grass."

Koji whispered, "And you're afraid that if you let me go, I'll tell people who you are and where your camp is. But I could never even find your camp. I won't tell!" He stopped walking and pressed Lord Udo's cloth to his forehead. "By the honor of this precious cloth, I promise!"

Spider pushed him forward through the darkening night.

Koji wrenched out of his grip, flung himself down before a roadside statue of Jizo, and prayed for help. The stone deity, chipped and scarred, held a lotus in both hands. Its face was childlike, its slight smile tender. A bag full of pebbles hung around its neck, and more were piled around its feet and on its head and shoulders. People would come to the little statue to pray for the souls of dead children. With each prayer, they left a pebble. *Did Mama, Papa, and Taro come here and pray for me?* Koji wondered. *Did they leave any of these pebbles?*

Spider drew Koji up onto his feet. "We have to go home."

"Your camp is not my home."

"We have to go anyway." Spider said it gently.

But as they made their way up the moonlit road, Koji alternated between trying to run away and flinging himself down in the dust to beg Spider to free him. By the time they reached the bamboo forest, Spider was livid again. Moving furiously, he ripped off the komuso wig and robe. Underneath, he had on the same dark outfit he'd worn when he captured Koji. He grabbed him by the collar and jerked him hard. "See that sapling, paddy frog?"

Koji glanced at it fearfully.

Spider whirled around. He whipped a steel star at the tree. It flickered in the moonlight as it shot forward and bit into the narrow trunk. Spider grabbed Koji and shook him. "Don't move or that sapling will be you," he spat. He retrieved the steel star, then buried the komuso disguise while Koji waited, shifting from foot to foot to show Spider he couldn't boss him around.

Spider leaped to his feet. He shoved Koji back against a mulberry tree. "I'm not going to tie you and hold a dagger to you like I did when I captured you. You're not worth the trouble." They stared at each other in hatred, then Spider added, "But do as I say or you'll be sorry. Now walk!"

Instead of starting away in front of Spider, Koji turned his head to gaze longingly past the bamboos toward the road to Kurikawa and Aokusai.

"I'm sick of you!" Spider lifted the star-shaped

blade. He slashed it down into Koji's arm. The skin split. Pain tore through Koji. He yelped. He clapped his hand over the gooey gash. But blood kept welling up between his fingers. It oozed down his arm. Koji was too shocked to move. When Spider yanked him forward, he stumbled ahead in numb silence.

Spider's face radiated fury as he slid between close bamboos and crouched to pass under low foliage. He knew every step. Now and then, he stopped to make hototogisu calls, and always, he was answered in the same way from within the black forest.

Spider swung around to Koji, who held his hand over his throbbing arm, slippery with blood. "You'll never escape from us. Quit trying!"

When Koji didn't answer, Spider threw back his shoulders. "I'm glad you know what we are. Next you'll tell us what you saw in the castle. Then we'll train you to become a *genin,* a field agent, like me. Personally, I think you'll never make it because no matter how long you let a potato grow, it will never become a hawk. But Grandfather thinks differently."

They hiked with twigs and leaves crunching underfoot. Koji was in shock. Become a ninja himself? Never! "You creep around so treacherously. Not like the honorable samurai," he said.

"Samurai!" Spider said with a sneer. "Do you long to be like that priggish, flute-playing Udo Norimaru?"

"Not him," Koji said, feeling helpless. "But at least the samurai are people. Everyone in the valley says you ninja—I mean, you grass people—are magical and evil, that you can walk on water, flow through walls, turn invisible . . . even fly. Is it true?"

"The magical part's true. Watch me fly now . . ." Spider leaped up, grabbed a branch, and swung himself to the next one with his arms outstretched. In the dim light, he did look as if he were flying.

He dropped to earth. "You think the samurai are honorable, and we're not? They pay some ninja clans—those with less integrity than we have—to 'creep around' doing whatever they think would dirty their own hands." He glanced at Koji with disgust. "Do you call that honor?"

Koji stood speechless. All his life, he had been taught to admire warriors of the samurai class. Yet he heard truth in Spider's words.

he next morning, Spider laid out the sketchy map of the castle on the grass. "Add anything you noticed," he commanded.

Koji gazed at the paper in silence. If Spider would like to know about anything he saw, surely he would most like to know about the new weapon. But what good would it do him to reveal the musket now? Yet there might come a time when the information would be precious.

Koji touched his arm where Spider had cut it. Clear Mist had bandaged the wound the night before, but it was still sore. "Why do you want to know what I saw in the castle, anyway?" Koji asked, although he thought he knew the answer.

"Why do you think?"

Koji was disgusted. He had hidden his firecrackers in one of the storeroom caves, but he wished he had them now. He wanted to light one and push it up Spider's nose. "You were in the castle with me, hidden somewhere," he said. "So think for yourself what the layout is like. I won't help you." It took all his courage to roll the map shut.

"Think hard before you make threats you are powerless to carry out," said a rasping voice from behind. Koji and Spider spun around together. Dark Fire sat on a nearby stump with his walking sticks on the ground beside him. On his knee, he balanced his pet cricket in its bamboo cage. He held one end of a long thread. The other end was tied around the leg of a crow with clipped wings. It hopped around, pecking at the ground.

Koji and Spider waited for Dark Fire's attention while he gave the string a harsh tug. He chuckled over the crow's antics as, cawing, it fell and fluttered its wings in a panic. After it finally calmed down, Dark Fire tugged the string again.

"I am becoming impatient with you, farm boy," he told Koji. He kept pulling the glossy bird closer. When it was near, he gently slid open the door of his pet cricket's cage. He tipped it up slightly and the cricket slid out onto the grass in front of the crow.

For a moment, the crow and cricket both stood motionless. Then the crow jerked its head forward and snapped up Dark Fire's beloved pet. With a twitching leg sticking out of its beak, the bird hopped away. Its head bobbed as it swallowed.

Dark Fire slid shut the door of the empty cricket cage. He folded his hands and turned back to Koji, who was stiff with horror. Dark Fire's eyes were flares as he rasped, "Unroll the map."

Koji was afraid to disobey, yet his hands were paralyzed.

"It is time for you to become one of us."

"I'll try to be like you," Koji said with a frantic bow.

Dark Fire looked down at his walking sticks. "Not like me. You are young and strong enough to complete missions, so you will begin as a genin like my grandson." He motioned toward Spider.

"Forgive my impoliteness at suggesting that I could be like you, our leader," Koji said, still trying to please the old man.

But Dark Fire's cheek twitched in irritation. "Groveling disgusts me. And I am not the true clan leader—the *jonin*. His identity is secret."

"But you alone communicate with him, Grandfather," Spider said proudly.

"That is my role as the number-one *chunin*." Looking down at his weak legs, Dark Fire sighed. "After all, I cannot be a training master like the other chunin."

Koji glanced at the empty cricket cage and the tame crow nearby. It hopped around, trying to bite off the string that was tied around its leg and snaked across the ground toward Dark Fire. Then he scanned the clearing full of people. *Does our jonin live here in the camp?* he wondered. *Does he know me?* But he glanced at the tail of the string, near Dark Fire's foot, and didn't dare ask.

Dark Fire seemed to guess Koji's thoughts. "You are unwise to wonder who our jonin is," he said. "Now draw!"

While Dark Fire watched, Koji forced his trembling hand to draw a few rooms, stairways, and large jars on the map. He pointed out the hall where O Kei had talked about a network of threads. But he paused before drawing the secrecy room, and as he held his hand motionless, Dark Fire nodded his approval.

"You will be a ninja until the day you die," Dark Fire said, and Koji laid down the brush. If Dark Fire was satisfied with what he had already drawn, perhaps it was safest to stop. "Continue being forthright with me and your death day may remain distant." Dark Fire gazed at Koji's bandaged arm. When Koji didn't explain the injury, the old man said, "Spend today with my grandson. If you learn a few things from him, tomorrow's challenge may be eased slightly. You see, you are ready to begin training."

"Training? I don't want—"

Dark Fire held up his hand for silence. "How long will you remain a bird who walks everywhere on its scrawny legs, never daring to try its wings? You will begin training tomorrow, whether you wish it or not. However, before you start, let me caution you that mastery of weapons and your arms and legs will only take you so far along the *ninjutsu* path. Our way is more about caring for each other, compassion, integrity." Dark Fire reached down for the end of the string. When he snapped it ever so slightly, the crow hopped

and fluttered its way back to him. "You see, compe-
tence and wisdom are found on different life journeys.
One does not lead to the other."

"Is that what I want?" Koji murmured. "Wisdom?"

As if the crow were a baby, Dark Fire reached down
and lifted it in his arms. "It's what you should want."
He motioned for Spider to take over with Koji and
hobbled away with the crow perched on his shoulder.

"Watch this." Grinning, Spider picked up the map of
the castle, folded it in half, and tore it down the middle.

"What are you doing?" Koji cried.

"Don't you realize we know every inch of the castle? We didn't wonder about the castle at all, but we
needed to test how you would respond when we asked
for your help. Would you tell us the truth about what
you saw or try to mislead us? Didn't you guess that
your assignment was not what it seemed?"

"No. How did I do?"

"Come on, let's fight." With his chest puffed out
importantly, Spider hoisted Koji up and pushed him to
one of the sparring circles. He sprang into the air as
flexibly as a shadow, raised his fists as he landed, and
began hitting out to warm up. Dancing just out of
reach, he lightly slapped Koji's cheeks. "Come on,
peppercorn, show me your spice!"

"No!" But Koji struck out with both fists. The
right connected, but it didn't slow Spider, whose fist
exploded in Koji's face. Koji fell and sat dazed. Blood
dripped into his mouth. Gulping, he pinched his
nostrils together.

"Weak little paddy frog," Spider muttered, kicking at Koji. He drew in a breath, then placed the sole of his left foot up against the inside of his right knee. With the palms of his hands together, he raised his arms over his head and stood motionless. He chanted under his breath with his eyes turned upward, then let his head fall onto his chest. He sprang out of position. "You're not ready for tomorrow," he warned Koji before trotting away.

Koji sat down near a scaling wall and, feeling glum, watched Raven Wing, Minnow, and Sky swarm up and down. Helped by clawlike pieces of metal strapped to their hands, they looked as comfortable as flies on the vertical surface. *Will Dark Fire expect me to do such impossible things?* he wondered anxiously.

"Koji." He turned to find Falcon kneeling behind him, looking as if he wanted to talk. But Spider ran up and grabbed Falcon by the shoulder as if to pull him away. Shaking him off, Falcon cast an indulgent smile up at him.

"It won't hurt if I talk to him, Spider. You don't understand how he feels." Gently, he added, "Koji, things will go easier for you if you accept being here."

Koji gazed at Falcon, realizing that if any ninja could become a trusted friend, it was him. He snatched a leaf off the ground and tore it to pieces. "I can't—I should be with my family."

"See? He says he refuses," Spider said as he sauntered off. "Falcon, you'll make him soft!" He snorted over his shoulder.

"You say you want to be with your family," Falcon

said to Koji. "Don't you realize that if you ever see them again . . ."

"Don't say 'if'!"

"When, then. Won't they be impressed to see you changed—so strong and competent?"

Koji glanced up, shocked and interested. He remembered a time, years ago, when a traveling peddler had been surprised to learn that he and Taro were twins; he assumed Koji was younger.

"No," Papa had said. "Koji is moments older. But he's immature compared to his brother, and that fools you. Look, can't you see that they're exactly the same height?"

Later that night, Papa and Mama murmured together, glancing at the twins now and then. Finally, Papa announced, "In the past, I've told you to try to act more grown up, Koji. But never mind. This way is best. Perhaps superstitious strangers won't even guess that you're twins."

Now as he gazed at Falcon, Koji wondered what it would be like to go home as a trained warrior, to meet strangers who assumed he was older than Taro.

"I don't know whether . . . ," Koji began. But was Falcon really someone in whom he could confide? He took in a deep breath. "I don't know whether my family could ever be proud of me again. I did . . . something bad."

"Mistakes are normal. Part of being alive."

"But I let down my whole family."

"Still, Koji, it's a hard heart that won't give the person he hurt a chance to forgive him."

s usual, the next morning a guard dragged Koji out of the dank prison cave where, night after night, he had hardly managed to sleep. But from then on, nothing was the same as on previous days. Koji started training to become a ninja.

He stood blinking into the dawn light that peeked down through the leaves. Before him, one of the ninjutsu masters, Sky's mother's cousin, was tying a rolled towel around his head as a sweat band. He was all slanted forehead and heavy brow and had a long, lippy mouth.

The man wore a scarlet loincloth and wide white stomach wrapper. Sweat glistened on his muscular arms and chest, which was tattooed with a warrior flourishing a sapphire-colored sword. The dragon under the warrior's foot breathed crimson flames. He gestured for Koji to show him his arm where

Spider had cut him. After examining the wound, he grunted. It would heal.

"Koji, you will train here, below this cryptomeria tree," he said, and laid one hand on the huge trunk. He looked as if he were soundlessly communicating with it.

Koji stared. The master was missing half of one finger.

"Frostbite," the master said tersely. "Now place your hand beside mine."

Feeling foolish, Koji pressed his hand against the trunk just above the sacred straw rope that encircled it.

"A powerful kami-sama dwells in this tree," the tattooed man said. "You, boy, feel nothing of the kami-sama's power. I can see it in your face. But in time you will."

A granite basin of water stood at the bottom of the tree. Following the master's instructions, Koji poured some of the purifying liquid over his hands, then filled his mouth with more and dribbled some onto the cords of his straw sandals.

"My ninja name is Wooden Fist," the master said when Koji had finished. "But like everyone here, I earned my name. And you must earn the right to use it. Until you do, you must call me *sensei* or 'First Master.' So we begin."

He bowed and Koji bowed back. But as Koji leaned over, he was struck hard on the shoulder. "Ow!" He leaped back.

First Master held a wooden training sword straight

out. "Your first lesson," he said, "is about *zanshin* . . . alertness. Never take your eyes off someone positioned to attack. Bow again."

Koji's shoulder throbbed. He was wary. The second time he lowered his head to bow, he didn't lean down so far. He tried to stay more watchful.

But First Master was tall and Koji couldn't help losing sight of his eyes and arms. *Thwack!* came the wooden sword down on him again. "It's not easy," First Master acknowledged. "But you're quick and light on your feet. Now hit me."

The praise pleased Koji. Despite feeling a little dizzy, he rubbed his hands together, made fists, and attacked First Master.

But the big tattooed man flung him back with one hand.

Time after time, Koji charged. Time after time, First Master blocked him. At last, Koji lay on the ground, exhausted.

First Master strode over to some weapons leaning against a cedar tree: a six-foot wooden pole, or *bo*, several chain-and-sickle contraptions, blowguns, hooked spears, and *nunchaku*. "Lesson two," he said, returning to Koji, bouncing the bo in his hands as if to test its weight. "No weapon is simply—or even foremost—a tool of punishment. First of all, it is the symbol of its wielder's spirit." He flicked his wrist and the pole sprang high up in the air. It whirled so fast that it didn't look rigid at all but like a graceful, arched snake.

It dropped neatly to stand upright in First Master's

hand. He tossed it to Koji and with his own hands empty, stepped into fighting stance. "Attack."

Waving the bo around wildly, Koji charged.

Gracefully, First Master knocked the pole out of Koji's hands. He twisted Koji and jerked his arm up behind his back. Koji danced around in pain. The First Master let go. Koji didn't know what the tattooed man did next, but somehow Koji went head over heels. He lay on the ground again, panting.

"As you continue working with these weapons," the training master said, "you will start to feel more comfortable with one than with any of the others. If we correctly identify that special weapon, then eventually you will feel energy—*ki*—flowing from it through you. You will resist evil best when you use that ki bearer because its spirit and yours will be intertwined." He peered at Koji. "Do you understand?"

"I think so, sensei," Koji said, still lying on the ground.

Wooden Fist loomed over him. "The wind tells rumors that you're determined to go back to your blood family."

His blood family . . . Koji's eyes fluttered shut as he remembered Papa, talking about clearing a spot in the forest where he could have a field that was not Lord Udo's, but his own. But Lord Udo's endless work never allowed time for that. Life only offered Papa planting, hoeing, weeding. Rice, rice, rice.

Koji remembered Mama, too, puny but working until she was ready to collapse, then feeding them and cleaning the house as well. And of course, Taro. Koji felt the Jizo against his pulsating heart. Taro had helped Papa carve it, only working on the left foot but precise about every cut. His carefulness paid off as always, and the left foot perfectly matched the right one.

Koji remembered how eager he'd felt as he butted between Papa and Taro, saying, "Let me whittle the left hand."

His father's hesitation had lasted for less than an instant, but Koji perceived it nevertheless. He was sure neither of the others noticed the pause, not Taro and not even Papa himself. But it was there.

So Koji laughed hard as he pushed the Jizo away. "I was joking," he said. "Who would want to cut cut cut on a piece of wood? How boring!" Later, when Papa was away at their field, Koji climbed up onto the roof of the house, broke twigs from the thatching—Papa would have spanked him for that one—and threw them down at his twin. "Carve that one, Taro," he called, and he was sure he sounded happy and light. "And that one. And that!"

And Taro, ever good-natured, responded by slinging handfuls of mud up at him, running whooping, having great fun. Taro, his mirror image, Taro, his best friend. His workmate and playmate and soulmate and rival.

"You are here to stay, Koji," he realized First Master was saying. "But you are free to choose your attitude. Now up."

Reluctantly, Koji got to his feet.

"You will be trained in eighteen disciplines." First Master listed them: sword handling, blade throwing, spying, escaping, disguise, spiritual growth. . . . "A ninja's first priority is to win without fighting. Preparation. Stealth. Deception. Subterfuge. Before a single blow is struck, these four tactics must be exhausted." With a stick, he drew a Chinese character in the dirt. "This one symbol means both 'strength' and 'nothingness.' Let it be your master. Now focus your energy . . . your ki." His eyes fluttered shut.

"Focus on what?" Koji asked.

First Master opened his eyes again. "On nothing. Only look within . . ."

At last, Koji's exhausting first day ended.

"Tomorrow we will discuss your training away from this practice ground," First Master said. "You see, a ninja who does not keep himself morally up-right during every moment may become physically skillful. But mentally, spiritually, he will never become a warrior."

He presented Koji with a lacquered box decorated with ninja in various fighting postures. It was filled with bladed steel disks like the ones Spider was always throwing. Some were star shaped; others were crosses, triangles, or darts. "These are called *shuriken,* Koji. They are the first weapons you must master. Hold them like this."

When First Master left, Koji stood turning a star in his hands. It was lightweight and keen. *I hope these blades turn out to be my ki bearers,* Koji thought as he practiced tossing them at a maple tree among the pines.

Suddenly, someone dropped onto him from the branches overhead. As Koji struggled, his attacker got him into a headlock. It was Spider.

For the first time, Koji took Spider's attack for what it was, an effort to practice sparring. *"Yaa-a-a-a—ai!"* he screamed. He clawed at Spider. But the bigger boy cartwheeled away. The move ended with a kick to Koji's backside. Koji fell headlong but scrambled up. He got a grip on Spider.

But Spider slipped out of his hold. He did a handspring and was behind Koji. He rolled between Koji's legs and leaped up in front of him. He grabbed Koji by the arms, then sat down abruptly, pulling Koji forward over his head. Koji landed and tried to roll away. Spider twisted and heaved Koji up. Koji threw his leg around Spider to bring him down. But Spider leaned over his head, hugged him around the torso, and flipped him again.

Koji fought hard. But using the ordinary kicks and punches he knew from wrestling with Taro, he was no match for the ninja. Finally, Koji lay on his back, panting. Spider stood with one foot on his chest. From above Spider's head, the sun glinted in Koji's eyes as if it were mocking him. Spider toed him in the ribs. "Come on, paddy frog. Grandfather says you're ready to stop sleeping in the prison cave."

Spider led Koji past the caves in the cliff to the far side of camp. Here, Koji had always thought the cliff wall was solid. But Spider got down on his hands and knees and pushed aside the wisteria vines to expose a gap almost too small to crawl into.

He disappeared through it, then called Koji onward. Koji squeezed into the narrow opening and squinted to adjust his eyes to the darkness. But because his body blocked the small entrance behind him, the space in front of him was darker than dark. It was saturated black.

"Come on," Spider's voice said from within the void, but Koji didn't dare go forward. *Anything could be in front of me,* he thought, *one of those thorny vines that booby-trap some dark passages, or even a bottomless pit.* "Koji . . . show me you trust me," Spider added in a wistful murmur.

Koji clenched his jaw, then crawled forward along an upward-sloping shaft. The stone walls stayed tight around him as he moved. Then from some distance ahead he heard an odd sound: a sudden low tone like a short gust of wind. A moment later, he emerged into a shadowy cavern. Spider was lighting a fire in the hearth.

This cave was smaller than any of the others Koji had seen, but tall enough to stand up in. Several narrow tunnels headed off from the back. The floor was carpeted with deep bearskins instead of straw mats, and all kinds of ninja weapons were strewn over them. Others hung from hooks forced into chinks in the walls and low ceiling, and a straw sparring dummy stood to one side. It was fancier than any of the ones used on the training grounds, with wooden sticks extending from it, for kicking and punching, Koji guessed. One area of the cave wall appeared to be composed more of clay than of stone, and a jumble of darts and shuriken were stabbed into it as if this were a spot for target practice. Nearby, two charcoal sketches had been drawn on the rough cave wall. One pictured a spider, the other a falcon.

Once the fire was crackling, Spider stood amid the chaos of weapons with his arms crossed. "What do you think?"

"It's amazing. What is this place?" Koji said in awe. "And listen to how my voice sounds. Almost ringing!"

"Something about this cave's shape makes that strange echo."

"What is the cave used for?"

"Falcon and I live here." Spider looked around with satisfaction. "We call it the ninja arsenal."

"Your parents let you live here alone?"

"My mother died when I was born. But I have my grandfather. And cousins and such."

"And your father?"

Spider looked away. "Gone. I don't want to talk about it."

"Sorry." Koji dropped his head, shocked to realize he wasn't the only one missing his parents.

"Besides, why shouldn't we live alone? We're full-grown ninja warriors. And the adults have no use for such a little cave. Most of them are too big even to crawl in here. The other boys live in a sort of dormitory cave near—"

"Yes, I've seen it. Will I start sleeping there now that I can leave the prison cave?"

"Do you want to? Or ..." Spider glanced at the low entrance as the same deep gust sounded that Koji had heard as he slid through the entry shaft. "Falcon's coming in."

A moment later, Falcon's face appeared from within the shaft. He smiled when he saw Koji. "I wondered when Spider would show you our hideout. Are you going to live here with us? We'll be the three ninja wild men!"

Koji glanced at Spider. Was there any chance he would agree to that? Instead of asking, he said, "Spider, what made those gusts of wind?"

"Come see," Falcon answered for Spider. He showed Koji that near one end of the shaft a trip wire crossed from side to side. It was attached to a thread that exited the shaft and connected to a network of other threads. The system set off bamboo chimes in the back tunnels. In the strangely shaped cave, they made the hollow sounds that told Spider and Falcon when someone was entering the ninja arsenal.

"Your most important training will take place in here," Spider said, "even though Wooden Fist won't ever know it." He lit a torch at the fire, then led Koji and Falcon through one of the exit tunnels into a back chamber.

"Let's show the paddy frog how this works," Spider told Falcon, who stepped up onto a stump set in the middle of the cavern. Spider snuffed the torch. Koji didn't know how Spider located him in the absolute darkness, but he did and placed a leather ball in his hand. "Hit Falcon with that," he said. "Knock him off the stump."

Koji squinted hard. "I can't even see where he is!"

Spider laughed. "That's the point. Training in complete darkness, your senses of hearing and touch become incredibly sharp. Training in this cave is why Falcon and I are the best ninja in our age group. Now go on, knock Falcon off the stump."

Koji raised his arm to throw.

"Not so fast, Koji," came Falcon's voice from out of the black. "Take your time. Listen first. This once, I'm speaking . . . giving you a hint where I am. Pay attention to where my voice comes from."

"But even if he didn't intentionally make any sound at all," Spider added, "to a trained ninja, there are always sounds."

Again Koji raised his arm, but this time he moved it in hairbreadths.

"Didn't Falcon say *slowly?*" Spider insisted. "You're like a herd of water buffalo! If you let him hear every move you make, he'll know exactly how to sway to dodge the ball."

Koji tried again. To avoid making the sounds that he couldn't hear but that they could, he lifted his hand only high enough to throw from his hip. He tried to pitch the ball in a controlled arc.

The ball thudded against the cave wall.

"Well . . . you missed," Falcon said, and Koji heard

him spring down off the stump. "But did you hear the swish of the ball as it passed me? It was a good fast toss, especially from so low."

"You know . . . I did hear that!" Koji said in amazement.

"Promising start," Spider admitted grudgingly.

Back in the main cavern, Spider and Falcon stretched out on bearskins with their hands behind their heads.

Koji looked from one boy to the other. "Did you really mean I can live here with you?" he asked. He didn't add that he couldn't wait to draw a symbol of himself . . . whatever he might eventually decide on . . . between the spider and falcon already on the cave wall.

"Of course!" Falcon said. "You're one of us now!"

Spider stretched out his foot and kicked at Koji. But he was smiling, too.

oji couldn't sleep. He still longed for his family; he still recoiled from becoming a ninja. But today's training session with First Master had been thrilling and now, to be living here with Spider and Falcon . . . !

After tossing fitfully for an hour, he sat up on his bearskin and looked around at the ninja arsenal. One torch burned through the night, and Koji noticed a dark ninja outfit, or *shinobi shozoku,* that hung from a pole leaning against the cave wall. He crept to it.

The shinobi shozoku was a key to the ninja world placed in his hand. Besides, he was starting to want to stay with the ninja long enough to find out which of the fascinating weapons would send its ki flowing through him. He found himself wrapping the long pieces around his legs to form pants. He tied them at his waist and pulled on the jacket, then wound the narrow cloth called a *zukin* around his head. Soon only his eyes were uncovered.

As he tied the gloves onto his hands, he heard a noise and swung around. Spider was staring at him, shocked. "How dare you put that on? Take it off," he whispered furiously. He glanced back toward where Falcon lay sleeping, then scrambled to Koji and wrenched the jacket off him.

"I'm sorry," Koji said.

"Leave it alone, you little . . ." Spider closed his lips tightly, apparently trying to control himself. He hung up the clothes again. "It was my father's." Spider flung himself back down to sleep, but Koji lay awake nearly till morning.

The forest camp began stirring at the hour of the tiger, when the only light swelled out from the fires of the night watch. All the ninja came together and faced their number-one chunin in rows. Toddlers played in front, understanding only enough to know that they must stay in their places. The tallest adults stood in back.

They faced Dark Fire together. Although Koji trained with the eight- and nine-year-olds, his spot here at the assembly was with the twelve- and thirteen-year-olds. He felt pleased that they willingly moved aside to make room for him. Even Raven Wing.

After breathing exercises, Dark Fire always posed a mystical riddle to them, such as, "Even a good thing isn't as good as nothing," or, "Scoop up water, and the moon is in your hands." They were to focus on this puzzle throughout the day, and in that way expand and purify their minds. After bowing to Dark Fire together, everyone clapped toward the rising sun.

For all the ninja, training began after breakfast, which was eaten casually around the camp. Koji worked with the eight- and nine-year-olds every morning, and Wooden Fist tutored him alone in the afternoons. Each day began with one or another specialist ninja teaching Koji and the others how to use common materials for ninjutsu. One day they learned to use smoke from smoldering rags to stop the flow of blood. Another day they collected soil from near their lavatory area back through the woods and scraped up ashes from the bonfires around the camp. Both the soil and ashes were used to create explosives. Koji's favorite lessons were when Clear Mist taught them how to form one or another of ninjutsu's nine mystical finger movements, like cuts through the air.

The day when Koji sparred and beat one after another of the eight- and nine-year-olds, First Master passed him into the ten- and eleven-year-olds' group. Eager to impress them, Koji clenched his jaw and his fists and charged First Master again and again like an attacking bull. Each time, First Master easily tossed him back.

Later, Koji and the others would run up and down felled trees positioned at various angles. The easiest ones were horizontal, the hardest almost vertical. For Koji, the toughest training exercise was *mudo,* when for hours he must remain still in whatever position First Master chose. He kept a bit of cloth in his mouth so that even his breath would be deadened. First Master seemed to know when Koji's cramped muscles were screaming in silent agony. Then the training master would lean close and whisper in the boy's ear, "A ninja is a warrior-mystic. He is *strong*. He *knows*. He *dares*. He is *silent*." Somehow, the four directives gave Koji the courage to persist.

As the weeks wore on, defiance didn't stop Koji's thin arms from growing sinewy or his legs from quickening. By the time summer ended, he could hang from a stout branch without moving from lunch time until supper. He hung by his fingers, high up in the branches with other young ninja suspended nearby. It was surreal, all of them dangling above the heads of people below.

He could break oak limbs with the side of his hand and creep along rice paper without tearing it. He could leap, then twist, kick, and knock over one straw dummy after another. He could back-flip all the way across the clearing without stopping even once.

When First Master passed him into the twelve- and thirteen-year-old training group, he ran his first race against Raven Wing. "Not bad, farmer," she said with a good-natured shrug when he won.

And his shuriken flew straight. Each time he threw one, a thrill would shiver its way up his spine. *That's the shuriken's ki flowing through me,* he thought, and kept the blades well polished. He could hardly wait for the moment when First Master would ask him if he'd identified his ki bearer.

But as he finished training one day in early autumn, Spider stopped before First Master. Bowing, he said, "Wooden Fist, you are called Koji's first training master. But in a sense, is it not true that I began training him even before you did?"

First Master smiled. "I suppose. You have been paired with him since the beginning. What is your point?"

"Normally, the first training master helps a new ninja select his ki bearer. May I help Koji choose his?"

First Master's eyebrows shot up in surprise. "Koji, it is an honor for someone who is not your obvious first training master to ask to help you identify your ki bearer."

Koji swallowed hard. "Yes, sensei," he said with his jaw clenched. After First Master had left him and Spider alone, Koji warned Spider, "I don't want your help picking my ki bearer. You and your tricks."

Spider looked at him with an innocence that was perhaps authentic, perhaps fake. "But I have a feeling about what you should have. I want to help."

"Leave my choice to me."

As the days passed, Koji began to appreciate the wild beauty of his forest home. Colors were sometimes very bright here, other times as soft as if he were seeing them through water. He especially liked digging his fingers into the moist earth—he relished its scent.

He loved the springy moss and pine needles underfoot. Minnows in the stream were like clippings of pale silk. The forest was alive; he sensed the presence of kami-sama who dwelt in the trees and rocks and even in the birds' chirping at dawn.

Spider and Falcon sometimes took him hunting. Koji would watch as the older boys shot pheasants with Falcon's ki bearer, the short ninja bow and arrow called *yumi* and *ya*. After several weeks of bored watching, Koji decided to show Spider once and for all which weapon must be his special one. He drew back his arm and whipped a shuriken at a rabbit. The steel star skimmed fast and straight. The rabbit dropped as it ran.

Spider and Falcon spun around to him together. For the first time, Koji saw admiration in Spider's eyes.

With a delighted laugh, Falcon thrust his bow into Koji's hands. "Give this weapon a try."

Spider's expression changed. "He's too small to handle it," he said, snatching the bow back.

"He won't be able to identify his own ki bearer if he doesn't try them all."

"No!" Spider said, frowning hard.

But Koji beamed gratefully at Falcon. *I wish you had captured me,* he thought. "Thanks, Falcon," he said. "But it doesn't matter. I already know what my ki bearer will be."

"Oh, do you?" Spider prompted with a sneer.

"Well . . . the shuriken."

Falcon laughed. "Spider wouldn't like that!"

"But . . . ?" Koji began.

Spider shoved his shoulder. "Shuriken are *my* ki bearers."

"Can't two ninja have the same ki bearer? There are more ninja than weapons, after all."

"Sometimes they can, Koji," Falcon said. "But Spider doesn't want you to have the same weapon he has. You'll have to keep searching for yours."

"Oh, no, he won't," Spider said. "I'm choosing it for him. And it definitely won't be shuriken."

s autumn progressed, Koji trained hard, some days with the twelve- and thirteen-year-olds, but more and more often tutored alone by Wooden Fist. He tried one weapon after another, an iron war fan one day, a fishnet or nunchaku the next. Always First Master asked Koji if he felt a particular connection to that day's weapon. But he never did. Although he knew that Spider wouldn't approve, he went on hoping that somehow shuriken would become his ki bearer.

First Master never taught to a strict schedule, warning the young ninja that schedules would make them rigid. Using all kinds of weapons, they sparred, climbed, and improved their weaponry, balance, speed, and stamina.

They trained in more subtle ways, too, all their techniques related to the eighteen disciplines of ninjutsu. Sometimes First Master led Koji's training group into the forest and translated the language of birds while they listened in wonder. Other days they would practice *kiai* shouting—expelling their breath in harmony with the universe—or they might use ninja skills to hide in the forest and seek each other out.

Some days, Koji worked in one of the several specialty caves. The camp cooks introduced him to the powders—some of them poisons—lined up in gourds against one cave wall. They also showed him how to detect the peculiar sheen of water that had been poisoned.

One training group or another was always climbing the cliff that bordered the camp. The younger children climbed horsehair ropes knotted at intervals and topped with grappling hooks. But the older ninja climbed using only spiked metal bands on their hands and feet.

During his free time, Koji liked to follow the stream up to the waterfall, where ninja guards hid high in the trees. Here he pretended to be alone, lying down beside the stream and trying to tickle the fish, just as he had done at the someru-ya.

One day as he sat there, a lasso dropped over his head and tightened around his chest. As he struggled, Spider ran out from behind some bushes, laughing. Falcon came along behind him.

"That wasn't funny, Spider," Falcon said as he pulled the lasso off Koji.

"What are you doing playing with fish, paddy

frog?" Spider scolded. "Don't waste your time. Catch dinner."

While Spider coiled the rope he had used as a lasso, Falcon attached string to a bamboo pole for Koji to fish with. He fastened a grasshopper onto it as bait. Soon the three boys sat fishing together, but Koji only snagged a frog. It kicked and convulsed as it revolved on the line.

"Your first time fishing and you caught something!" Falcon said as he worked to release the frantic frog. He had a way of pointing out any bright speck in a predicament.

"Paddy frog's caught one of his own kind!" Spider cried, digging his fingernails into the soft underbelly of one of his own fish. Deftly, he slid his fingers along its length on both sides. A flick of his wrist sent the innards flying, and the fish was gutted. "You'll never be able to do that, paddy frog!"

Koji was furious. Once they were back at camp, he went to his hidden firecrackers. He tied them in a cloth waterproofed with lacquer and returned to the stream with the bundle. He pushed a lit sliver of wood through the mouth of the packet and flung it into the water.

For a moment: nothing. Then the firecrackers exploded. Underwater, the blast made no sound. But a section of the stream leaped straight up. As the water plummeted to splash back into the stream bed, a dozen or more dead fish of all kinds floated up onto the water's surface.

Koji collected all the fish, strung them onto a line, and ran down the mountain to the training camp. He entered it with his long string of fish trailing down his back.

People stared as Koji steamed across the clearing to Spider, who was training with a handled chain. Koji hurled the string of fish down before Spider, then reveled in his look of shock.

Behind Spider, Koji noticed a villager striding through the dry autumn grass into camp. Koji knew him from Kurikawa. He sometimes sold turtles in jars and sparrows in bamboo cages at the village shrine for people to free for good luck. Until now, Koji had thought he was hunchbacked. But today he looked as agile as Spider. Confused, Koji started toward the man.

Spider whipped his chain out and wrapped it around Koji's leg—just enough to unbalance him without pulling him off his feet. "I see you recognize him," he said.

"Yes," Koji said, shaking his leg free of the chain. "What's he doing here? He's not a ninja."

"Yes, he's a genin. We need contacts in your world, so some of us live in the valley. How else could we survive up here?"

"By making cloth from nettles, building homes in caves . . ."

"Partly, yes. But our valley contacts get us food and clothes too elaborate to make in the sewing cave. Information, too, but getting that can be complicated."

"I can't believe it. Someone I know from the valley comes in and out of the camp freely?"

Spider narrowed his eyes at Koji. "I see what you're hoping. Don't be a fool. The fact that he comes here doesn't mean you can sneak out in his pocket."

As he gazed at the villager, Koji remembered an earlier conversation with Dark Fire. "Didn't your grandfather tell me that he isn't the highest leader of our clan—the jonin?"

"No, Grandfather isn't the jonin, but the two of them plan our missions together. Secretly, for security. Why?"

"Because the secret jonin must come to camp at least sometimes to talk to Dark Fire. Maybe that villager is more than a genin. Maybe he's our jonin."

"Wrong! The jonin would never come to this camp. Too risky! He and Grandfather never meet. They wouldn't know each other if they came face-to-face. They communicate through a series of people. Each one knows only two people in that chain, the one who tells him information and the one he then tells. Not even Grandfather knows who the jonin is. I don't want to know, and you shouldn't either. Too dangerous! But I can promise you that that villager is an ordinary genin, like me."

"I still don't understand how a villager can be a ninja."

"None of us are what we seem. Won't you ever get that through that pumpkin you call your head?" Spider turned away for a moment. When he looked back, it was as if he had slipped on a disguise without changing his clothes. He stood hunched over. His legs trembled. Even the muscles of his face seemed to droop. Koji would have sworn that his skin was grayish and that he had dark circles under his eyes. Then he turned away again, and when he looked back at Koji, he was himself.

As Koji stared, fascinated, Spider motioned to him. "Come with me—we need to talk to Grandfather about something."

"What?" Koji asked nervously, but Spider only picked up Koji's string of fish and carried them to the cooking cave as if he'd caught them himself. Koji trailed after him to Dark Fire's cave.

Koji knelt next to the cushion that faced the chunin. Spider knelt beside him as Dark Fire folded his hands, then turned his reptilian glance toward Koji. "My grandson has asked me to be present while he presents you with your ki bearer."

Shock flooded Koji. *Surely, Spider wouldn't choose my weapon without consulting me,* he thought, *and not in front of Dark Fire himself, so that I have no choice but to accept. He isn't that mean.*

But I did mention the shuriken to Spider, he remembered with relief. *He knows which weapon I want. He must have reconsidered and decided we can both have the same ki bearer.*

Spider reached into the chest pocket of his kimono. Koji watched, holding his breath, as Spider drew forth . . .

. . . a bamboo flute.

For a moment, Koji was too shocked to respond. Then he pushed it away in disgust. Suddenly, having the shuriken as his ki bearer wasn't important. He wanted any weapon, anything but a piece of bamboo. "That's no weapon!" he burst out to Dark Fire.

Dark Fire dashed his hand through the air in irritation. "You respond to such a profound gift with loathing?"

Gritting his teeth, Koji bowed his head to Dark Fire, then snatched the flute from Spider. But in a last struggle for help, he begged, "Sensei, I have never in my life touched a flute. I don't know if I can even learn to play."

"If my grandson has chosen wisely and if his motives are pure, you will indeed learn to play and play well."

"But you said a ninja chooses his own weapon," Koji said, ashamed that he sounded desperate. He thought of the incredible array of weapons strewn on the floor of their ninja arsenal cave. He would have willingly taken any one of them as his ki bearer.

"Indeed, a ninja does usually sense for himself which weapon bears his ki. But as I've told you before, nothing is inflexible here in the forest. Certainly not rules. No, your mentor has spoken, and his decision will stand." Dark Fire cast a cool glance at Spider. "If you cannot or will not learn to play, it will reflect badly on him."

Koji held out his arm to keep the flute away from his body.

Dark Fire sighed. "Kojiro, will you never offer me

proof that I was wise to keep you alive, that you will become a ninja whom I can be proud to add to our clan?"

Koji seethed like the embers glowing orange in the brazier. It was bad enough for Spider to force a flute on him instead of a weapon, but he had even manipulated things so that Dark Fire scolded him.

On the other hand, Koji thought, *if I can twist things my way and regain Dark Fire's approval, then he might still let me exchange this flute for shuriken.* Surely, this was the moment he'd waited for, the moment to tell Dark Fire about the musket. "You know, sensei," he said with his heart fluttering, "you asked me what I saw in Crane Castle. Well, I saw Udo-sama himself!"

Dark Fire's eyes widened. "You came face-to-face with that scorpion and escaped without being stung? If only everyone in this valley could be so lucky! Lord Udo has mangled the samurai warrior's honor code into cruelty and abuse. A *daimyo* is supposed to protect his farmers as a father looks out for his family. Instead, he torments them."

"He's evil!" said Koji.

"Yes. But you, little farm boy, can help us destroy his power. If we do that, we'll help every farm family in the valley."

Hope surged up in Koji. *Even my family,* he thought.

ark Fire clapped, and in response, three ninja came into the cave. They knelt near Spider and Dark Fire.

"I did not summon you here only about the flute," Dark Fire told Koji. "These other chunin and I wish to speak to you about something important."

Koji wasn't ready to give up this chance to impress Dark Fire and win shuriken as his ki bearer. In fact, now he could impress three more chunin at the same time. "Lord Udo wasn't the only high-ranking samurai I saw in the castle. I met a visitor who showed—"

"Does he speak the truth, Grandson?" Dark Fire interrupted, his head snapping around to Spider. "Whom did he meet?"

"Koji *was* in the reception hall," Spider admitted.

Dark Fire jerked his head forward toward Koji,

just as the crow had jerked its head to eat Dark Fire's cricket. "I commanded you to tell us all you saw in the castle, and you did not mention seeing an important samurai visitor?"

As he knelt, Koji leaned forward in such a low bow that he pressed his forehead down into the dirt. "Sensei, you asked me about the building. Walls and things. I didn't realize . . ."

"All right," Dark Fire said in a tight voice. "That was when you were new here. But nothing similar must happen again."

"This samurai wasn't by any chance rather flat-faced?" one of the ninja behind Dark Fire asked Koji.

"Yes! Flat-faced with teeth like a horse."

Dark Fire ran his bony forefinger along the top of his cricket's empty cage beside him on his tea tray. "We know him. He is one of the *shogun's* generals. So he paid a visit to our scorpion, eh?" He tossed the empty cage toward the cave wall. "You see, Lord Udo longs to be the most powerful man in Japan. That role actually goes to Ashikaga Yoshiharu—the shogun."

"Most powerful? Not more than the emperor?" Koji asked.

"On military matters, yes. Far more powerful. Now. What did the shogun's general say to our scorpion?"

Koji squared his shoulders. "They stopped talking when I came in, but that flat-faced samurai showed me something."

"Did he? What was it? A painting? A pet?"

"No. A new weapon."

Dark Fire's lizardlike eyes turned greedy and he seized Koji. "No!" he rasped. "You would have mentioned that at once!"

"I told you, I thought you meant the castle layout!"

"Then Lord Udo is not the only fool in Japan!" Dark Fire said, tossing Koji back with a snort of disgust.

As before, Koji pushed his forehead onto the dirty cave floor. "I'm sorry!" he said, then dared to peek up at Dark Fire. "It shoots firecrackers."

"Sketch the weapon," Dark Fire commanded, pointing at a patch of grit at his feet.

Koji knelt in the dirt and used the flute to draw.

"Kojiro! I am not yet finished feeling angry with you, and already you treat your precious gift like an old stick?"

Glaring at Spider, Koji put down the flute. Instead, he drew with a stone as the ninja stood around him, watching. When he finished, Dark Fire studied the picture in silence.

"I've heard about this new weapon. There are only a few in Japan. Barbarians brought them in."

"Udo-sama and the flat-faced samurai want to make more weapons like it."

"More?" Dark Fire sounded alarmed.

"But there's a tricky part."

"Show me on your drawing."

"This. It's part of the firing mechanism."

"Yes, that might well give a blacksmith trouble."

"I held the weapon myself. Like this." Koji turned

the flute and positioned it against his shoulder as if it were the musket. "It wasn't loaded, though. No firecracker."

"Good boy." Dark Fire snapped his fingers, and one of the chunin rubbed his foot through the picture to obliterate it. "In the future, never keep such information from me. Not for a moment." Dark Fire's sly little eyes shifted from the cave floor to Koji. "I wonder, do you feel ready to help us . . . as a ninja?"

"As a . . . yes! I want to use my new skills," Koji said, flexing his hands while his flute lay in the dirt. "If shuriken were my ki bearers, I could help you more."

"No. Remember, the work of a ninja is mainly espionage. The greatest warriors conquer without fighting." Dark Fire nodded toward Koji's fists. "You look as if mainly you want to wrestle. Is that why you are willing to help me? To have fun sparring? Not to support the ninja cause?"

Feeling uncertain, Koji let his hands fall open.

"I have been told that at Crane Castle you got over the outer wall without equipment," Dark Fire went on.

Spider crossed his arms and leaned back comfortably against the cave wall. He looked smug, and Koji felt himself blushing.

"The bamboo you climbed was planted too near the wall," Dark Fire added. "It's a weak spot in the castle defenses. But that attempt to flee . . . Are you loyal to us now?"

"Yes, sensei!"

"Hmm," Dark Fire murmured, frowning.

"Sensei, don't doubt me! You know I long for my family. Wouldn't I do anything to help you destroy the man who takes the food from their mouths?"

"I believe you would," Dark Fire said. "Show Wooden Fist this tree. Future missions will be easier if I know about such weak spots in the castle defenses. Can you swim?"

"No, sensei. I'm sorry!"

"Wooden Fist can find another way for you to cross the moat. You see, he will command this mission to evaluate the weakness in the castle defenses. And Grandson, since you linked your karma with Kojiro's by saving his life, you will accompany him." Dark Fire clapped once. "Then it is settled. This mission will take place the next time many castle guards are away."

"How can you find out when they'll be away?" Koji asked.

A slight movement of Dark Fire's shoulders warned Koji not to ask such questions. "Now go," he said, flicking his fingers.

Koji bowed and began backing away from Dark Fire and the assembled ninja. But Dark Fire called him back.

"A warning," he said. "In the future, you will tell me anything and everything you happen to learn about weapons, samurai . . . events outside this camp. Even seemingly minor ones."

"Yes, sensei."

"If your behavior on this mission displeases me, I fear I must displease you, too." He glanced at the empty cricket cage, upside down and discarded in the cave shadows. "I miss my little dear one every single day," he murmured with distant sorrow in his eyes. "She was precious to me."

fter speaking with Dark Fire, Koji went straight to the ninja arsenal and threw the flute down among the weapons strewn over the cave floor. He kicked at it in frustration. If he had a ki bearer like Spider's shuriken or even Falcon's yumi and ya, he would feel proud to be going on his first mission. But he had no weapon, only a useless piece of bamboo.

When he went back outside, he found Spider searching for him. "Come on," the bigger boy said. "I'll show you our usual pre-mission diet." He taught Koji how to lay out raw rice on a flat rock and, after the sun had heated it, to rub it between his hands and eat it. "Cooked food saps your energy and stamina," Spider explained, obviously feeling important. "Intuition, too."

For the next several days, Koji ate only raw foods: nuts, bamboo shoots, rice, and sliced sweet potato. At last the evening of the mission arrived. An hour before they were to leave, Koji sat grinding the disappointing food between his teeth. Spider handed him a package wrapped in white paper.

"Last time you gave me something, it was that worthless flute," Koji grumbled. "I don't want anything else from you."

"The flute isn't worthless. Anyway, you will want this."

Koji peeked inside. Spider was right, and he hugged the package to his chest. "My own shinobi shozoku. Thank you, Spider," he breathed, genuinely liking the bigger boy for the first time.

Spider's expression turned sour. "You have the wrong idea—it isn't yours to keep. Falcon is letting you borrow his outgrown one for this mission."

Disappointed, Koji dropped his chin onto his chest. "Oh."

"Surely you didn't think you'd earned it? You've done nothing."

"No one told me I had to earn it," Koji said, embarrassed.

Spider flipped his hand at the shinobi shozoku. "Put it on, paddy frog. Then meet us in the cave with the altar."

A few minutes later, Koji hurried across the camp, quiet now at night. He met Spider and First Master in a cave where Clear Mist stood beside a crude shrine. Candlelight flickered weirdly across their faces. Koji knew that wearing Falcon's shinobi shozoku, he looked like a real ninja. But after days of the inadequate food of the pre-mission diet, he had passed beyond hunger to lightheadedness. He felt more like fainting than going on a mission. Yet, "That feeling will make you superalert," First Master said. "It may save your life."

They prayed to Amida Buddha for strength and courage. Clear Mist watched Koji inhale and exhale, making sure that his ki was flowing freely. To help them lock their minds, she chanted while they drew in the air the mystical finger movements, called *kuji-kuri,* of five horizontal and four vertical finger lines.

"*Ganbaro!*" they cried. "We'll stand firm and never give up!"

And they were ready.

Clouds covered the moon, darkening the night as First Master and Spider stepped out of the cave with Koji between them. Now over his shinobi shozoku Koji wore a string of shuriken around his waist and a ninja sword, or *shinobi gatana,* strapped to his back. A dagger hung from his sash, along with a hooked rope, or *kaginawa,* and two bamboo containers. One held pepper to throw into an enemy's eyes. The other was filled with water chestnuts in their hard, pointy shells. He could toss them behind him to hurt pursuers' feet.

They had turned to start down the mountain when they heard "Wait!" Dark Fire limped toward them on his two walking sticks. Minnow came along behind him, carrying a broad, hollowed-out walking stick and a length of cloth waterproofed in lacquer. "Kojiro, I know I told you this mission would be simple—only showing Wooden Fist the bamboo tree near the castle wall. But I wonder if you can handle something more complex?"

"I can!"

Dark Fire's questioning glance went from Koji to Wooden Fist. "I need that musket he saw. Undoubtedly, Udo-sama sleeps with such a precious item right beside him."

The training master glanced at Koji. "He is well trained and brave. We'll do our best to get the musket."

"Good!" Dark Fire said, motioning to Minnow. She handed First Master the walking stick and cloth. "You can use these to hide it."

They became shadows among shadows and, with stealthy cross steps that left no footprints, soundlessly glided down the mountain. Koji and the others fused with dark forms that by day were bushes or boulders, then detached from them as gently as drops of thick lacquer dripping from a brush.

First Master led them through the forest to an abandoned hut near the castle. He had spread lard on his ankle, and before opening the hut's door, he rubbed the grease on the rusty hinges to silence them.

They crept inside. Spider and First Master scratched around in a corner, their shadows flickering against the walls. Under the pebbles and dirt on the earth floor, the edges of a hatch appeared. Wooden Fist opened it while Spider drew a small length of bamboo out of one of his pockets, then took off his shinobi shozoku. From a dark corner he retrieved a piece of waterproofed cloth that

Koji supposed he had hidden there earlier. After wrapping it around his folded clothes, he tied the package to his shoulder. He dropped the walking stick ahead of him into the black hole. Then, wearing only his loincloth with the piece of bamboo tucked into it against his back, he lowered himself into the shaft. After Koji and First Master also lashed their outer clothing onto their shoulders, the training master motioned for Koji to follow Spider into the gaping hole.

Down there, it was as black and empty as the pupil of an eye. Sweating furiously, Koji reared back. "Do I have to?" he whispered.

"Yes. This tunnel will take us all the way to the moat, right outside the castle walls." First Master gripped him by the shoulders and pitched him feet first into the cavity. A short distance down, Koji crouched at the entrance to a cramped tunnel. First Master gave him a little kick from above, and Koji inched forward. The training master slid down the shaft behind Koji and pulled the cover shut.

Not even the ninja caves' darkness was this dense. The tunnel walls squeezed Koji, but he forced himself to crawl ahead. The only sounds were the scrapings of Spider's hands and knees.

There's no air. I'm in my grave, Koji thought.

Something hurt his foot. It felt like a biting rat. He tried to scream, but panic clogged his throat. He couldn't breathe. "Help!" He clawed at the tunnel wall. "Help!"

"Koji!" Coming out of the darkness, First Master's

sharp voice paralyzed him. "Remember. A ninja dares."

Koji realized that the pain in his foot was only First Master, silently urging him forward by pinching his ankle. His horror smoothed out a little. He stopped gouging at the wall.

With terror still gripping him by the throat, he went on creeping forward. He thought he'd gone miles when fresh air rushed in at him. Ahead, Spider was silhouetted, slipping out into the circle of moonlight.

The tunnel had ended at the moat's steep bank. Koji heard the lapping water before he saw it below. He pushed aside some bushes that hid the tunnel's opening and peeked out at the narrow mud bank and moat just below him. He tilted his face to the sky and sucked in cool autumn air.

Spider was already treading water in the moat. His presence disturbed frogs, and Koji watched him sprinkle over the water a powder Koji had helped him make of crushed nettle thorns, centipede, and miso. It would keep the frogs croaking normally.

Behind Koji, First Master piled up a few rocks to cover the tunnel's exit. Koji slipped into the muddy water. It was icy. While he caught his breath after the shock, the training master slid into the moat, too. He guided Koji's hand to the side of the moat. Many weeks ago, a preparation team of ninja had installed a hand grip under the water's surface for missions like this one. Holding on to the grip, Koji treaded water and waited for Spider to tie a rope around his own waist. Spider handed the rope's other end to First Master, then silently dove just below the moat's surface and sliced through the water with the rope stretching out behind him. The only sign of him was the tip of the bamboo through which he breathed.

Soon Spider jerked on the rope to let First Master and Koji know he had reached the far side of the moat and had tied his end of the rope securely. First Master tied the other end of the rope to the grip. Below the water's surface, the attached rope stretched from one side of the moat to the other. First Master fastened a stiff cloth, thinly covered with lacquer, around Koji's mouth and nose. He pulled only the hems of the cloth tightly against Koji's cheeks to form a loose bag. Firmly, he placed Koji's hands on the rope and motioned for him to slide across the moat hand over hand.

Koji pushed off and sank down into the murky water. Here it was hushed. The lacquered cloth around his face created a balloon of air that swelled and collapsed a little as he breathed. The face cloth was all that kept him from drowning, and it was flimsy. Water began seeping in around its edges as he kicked his legs and pulled himself along the rope. Water plants dragged against him and clung. His hands hurt from clenching the rope so hard.

Terror chased him onward. Once he reached the far side of the moat, Spider's strong arms found him in the black water. Spider helped Koji crawl up onto the bit of land between the moat and the castle wall.

Gasping for air, Koji tore the lacquered cloth from

his face. Water streamed off him. Hidden in the shadows, he and Spider put on their shinobi shozoku as First Master emerged from the moat. He dressed, too, then coiled the wet rope over his shoulder.

The castle's outer wall loomed above them. It was made of large stones with spaces in between that would serve as hand and toe holds. They flung up ropes with grappling hooks on the ends, then scaled the wall and dropped to the other side. While Spider went on ahead to make sure that the musket was by Lord Udo's side, Koji and First Master looked for the bamboo Koji had climbed to cross the castle wall. They slipped from shadow to shadow, crouching now and then to look like stones. When they finally found the tree, First Master scanned the area thoughtfully, then nodded.

Koji beamed. First he had told Dark Fire about Udo-sama's musket, and now he had shown First Master a weak spot in Crane Castle's defenses. Twice he had helped fight evil in a way that no other ninja could have done.

irst Master and Koji crept to their ren-
dezvous place with Spider, near some wooden storage chests in the lower part of the castle. Footsteps
sounded from down the corridor. *It's Spider,* Koji
thought, stepping out of his hiding place. But First
Master pulled him back. One glance at his training
master's face told Koji what was wrong. Spider's
approach would be soundless. This had to be someone else.

The footsteps drew nearer. Koji stayed hidden,
but the space behind the storage chests was too narrow for the training master. Koji saw pain flash across
his face as he disjointed both shoulders and melted
into a pillar. What had been First Master in a shinobi
shozoku became nothing but a darker shape within
the pillar's shadow. He might as well have been invisible.

Down the hall, a nobleman appeared from around the corner. It was Udo Norimaru, the young man who had pushed Koji into the reception hall with Lord Udo. Norimaru pranced nearer, then swept past First Master so closely that their sleeves brushed together. But he was unaware of the ninja touching him. *Vindication!* Koji thought. *He is a fool.*

As soon as Norimaru had passed, Koji felt a touch on his shoulder. He spun around. Spider was crouched behind him. All this time he had been hiding with Koji, as close to him as a scabbard to its sword. Koji felt stupid. He was no better an observer than Lord Udo's pompous son.

First Master melted away from the pillar. He sprinkled ashes on the floor. Communicating silently for as much of the conversation as possible, Spider drew symbols in them with his finger, then wiped them away with the side of his hand and made more. They meant nothing to Koji, but obviously, the others were deciding what to do next.

"Udo-sama's asleep in his room," First Master finally whispered to Koji. "If he has the musket with him, Spider will retrieve it."

"But I need you, Koji," Spider added, "to deepen his sleep. You're the right size. If . . . ?" He glanced at the training master questioningly.

First Master nodded. Koji could handle the task. Explaining Koji's mission in whispers, he gave the boy a silk thread with a small wooden weight attached to one end and an emptied eggshell. A tiny hole drilled into the top was sealed with wax. Liquid sloshed around inside the shell. "Sleeping potion," First Master explained.

They slunk through the castle to a spot where First Master hoisted Koji into the rafters. But as he started to crawl up into them, Spider handed him a pellet of what looked like pressed herbs. "If you're caught," he whispered, "swallow that."

In the mountain camp, Koji had learned about the compressed food pellets a ninja took on long journeys. Still, he was surprised that Spider, of all people, cared whether he felt hunger pangs. Perhaps he wasn't all bad.

Koji dropped the pellet into one of his many pockets before squinting across the open beamwork that disappeared into darkness. Shadows and cobwebs loomed ahead, and the distance to the floor, if he fell, was dangerously far.

Koji crept forward along the beams. *I'm helping on a mission that neither Spider nor even First Master can complete without me,* he realized. *I am well trained. Wait until Taro sees me!*

After he'd crossed the distance of several rooms, the ceiling changed from heavy beams to thin oak boards, strong but creaky. Koji crawled over them carefully and reached the spot First Master had described. He was at the edge of one of the oakwood panels that formed a hollow square around the ceiling of Udo-sama's sleep chamber. Above him, on a second, higher ceiling over the center of the room, was a mural of dragons playing among clouds.

Careful not to topple over, Koji craned his neck forward to peek down over the edge. From this spot he must perform the dripping thread technique on Lord Udo below, lying asleep on his back with his mouth gaping. A luxurious silk quilt was pulled up to his chin. A wooden pillow propped up his head so that he wouldn't roll over in his sleep and ruin his carefully oiled topknot.

Next to him lay his long and short samurai swords. The very musket Koji had held in his hands stretched out between them.

With his heart drumming, Koji plucked the silk strand from his pocket. He shifted slightly, moved his hand forward . . . back . . . positioned it above Udo-sama's mouth. Then with trembling fingers, he lowered the thread.

The dangling thread swayed left and right. Only when it was directly above Lord Udo's open mouth did Koji bite the wax plug off the top of the eggshell. He dribbled drop after drop of the liquid onto the thread, then blew on it to force the droplets down. They rolled along the thread toward the samurai's mouth.

The first drops rolled down the thread and then dripped into Lord Udo's mouth without mishap. But as the last of the liquid trickled onto his tongue, he smacked his lips as he slept. His breath caught between snores and he started waking.

Frantically, Koji reeled up the silk thread. In his hurry, his knee shifted and made a sound. At the thump on the ceiling, Lord Udo sat up. Koji jerked himself back from the edge of the oak frame and pulled up the last bit of thread. He dared to peek over the edge and saw Lord Udo looking around groggily. But after a few moments during which Koji held his breath, paralyzed, Udo-sama collapsed and went back to sleep.

First Master had told him to stay in place until he saw Spider complete his part of the mission. Hunched back away from the edge of the oak frame, Koji stayed motionless until he began feeling bored. Then he fingered the gritty compressed food pellet in the pocket of his shinobi shozoku. Spider had told him to eat it only if he was caught. But he was so hungry.

As Koji started to pop the pellet into his mouth, he heard a sound in the room below, a sound so slight that only a ninja would hear it. Holding the pellet in his hand, he peered over the edge of the ceiling's oak frame. In the moonlit room below, Spider was sprinkling a minuscule amount of rice powder over Lord Udo's face. Koji knew the trick: a person sleeping only lightly or faking sleep would feel even this light sift of powder. His flickering eyelids would give him away while the ninja was poised to attack.

But Koji's sleeping potion had done its work. Lord Udo kept sleeping, and Spider carefully lifted the musket from between the two swords. As he stole away, Koji replaced the pellet in his pocket. He crawled back over the oak ceiling, then across the beams to the place where First Master had lifted him up into the rafters. Quietly, he dropped to the ground.

He crept through the silent, nighttime castle. He

hid within shadows, clung to walls, and dashed between pillars to make his way back to where he was to meet the other ninja. He'd almost reached the spot when, from behind, someone tugged on his shoulder. He whirled around, horrified.

Spider. He pulled Koji into a shadowy alcove and showed him the musket. Looking proud, he wrapped it in the waterproofed cloth Minnow had given him and stuffed it into the broad, hollowed-out walking stick. The stock stuck out of the top, but wrapped in cloth, it was disguised.

In silence, they recrossed the moat.

"I did well, didn't I, Spider?" Koji asked when they had reached safety in a grove of cherry trees outside the castle walls.

"You didn't bring your flute," Spider grumbled.

"What for?"

"I don't know, but once you have a ki bearer, you never—"

"I did do well," Koji cut him off. "Where's First Master?"

"He'll see us back at camp. But he asked me to give you this." Spider put one grain of rice into Koji's hand. It had been dyed green and baked hard.

"What does it mean?" Koji asked.

Spider smiled. "He's telling you that you've earned the right to call him by his ninja name, Wooden Fist."

Koji closed his fingers around the precious green grain of rice.

Spider knelt beneath one of the cherry trees and

lifted a broad stone. Under it he placed three more grains of rice, one red, one blue, and one yellow. "Wooden Fist will check here," he told Koji as he replaced the stone, "and know we're out safely."

"Wooden Fist," Koji murmured, trying out the sound. He wished he had a ninja name, too, to tell Taro when he saw him again.

As Spider straightened up, brushing dirt off his hands, Koji started out toward the dark road. But Spider caught hold of his arm and yanked him back.

"Let go!" Koji said, swatting at him.

"Don't step onto the road until I say you can," Spider warned.

"Or what? Dark Fire wouldn't let you harm me now that—"

"Now that what? Do you think wearing a borrowed shinobi shozoku makes you one of us? Take it off. If we put on kimono, we can walk openly."

"Maybe my clothes don't make me one of you, but Dark Fire sent me on this mission, didn't he?"

"You think Grandfather suddenly trusts you because you've learned a few tricks and sparring moves?"

Koji unwrapped his zukin in silence, then took off his shinobi shozoku. His chest felt stormy. "He has trusted me since I told him about the musket."

Spider held out his hand. "Give me that pellet."

"I'm hungry. I'm going to eat it now."

"Eat it? It's poison! What did you think?"

"It's compressed food," Koji said, confused.

"You idiot."

Filled with rage, Koji lifted his fists to fight.

Spider slapped down his hands. "A paddy frog with fangs. That's a new beast!" He snatched the shinobi shozoku from Koji and fished the pellet out of the pocket. "For now, we'll hide our clothes here." Then he added, "You think you're Grandfather's darling because you finally admitted to seeing that musket? You waited a long time before you told him about it. And *I* know you're still leaving something out."

Koji couldn't guess what Spider meant, but he felt uneasy. "It's hard to remember everything," he muttered.

Spider knelt to finish burying their clothes. "Is it hard to remember the secrecy room Jade Bat showed you?"

Koji felt the blood drain from his face. "I *did* start telling him about it. But he seemed to have heard enough, and—"

"You look pale," Spider interrupted, standing up and offering Koji his arm for support. "Are you all right? There's a safe house nearby where you can rest."

"No, I'm fine. But you know about that secrecy room?"

"I told you I was invisibly with you," Spider declared. "Don't you listen?" Wearing a kimono and carrying the heavy walking stick, he strolled out onto the road in thoughtful silence. Koji dragged along at his heels.

"Would it help if I tell him about the secrecy room now?"

"It doesn't matter anymore—that mission was only a test. But telling us about the musket helps us tremendously."

"Was this mission one more trick?" Koji asked bitterly. "Was Lord Udo himself in on it?"

Spider gave a noncommital lift of his eyebrows. "I'm too heavy to crawl over those ceiling beams, and so is Wooden Fist."

"Still . . . that poisoned pellet. You weren't sure about me."

Spider laughed. "Change comes slowly. Be patient."

redawn light bathed them as they walked in the lantern's glow. No one would have guessed that a strange new weapon was hidden inside Spider's thick walking stick.

Kurikawa lay ahead. Koji suddenly knew what he missed most: the touch of Mama's gentle hands washing his face. She still did it for him and Taro, even as she told them they were too big.

He wondered whether she thought he was dead. For the first forty-nine days after he'd disappeared, maybe she watched the roof ridge, envisioning his soul there whenever a breeze blew. People said dragonflies were the souls of the dead. When Mama saw one, did she wonder if it was him?

Longingly, he gazed up the road past the arched bridge that led over the river to Kurikawa.

But something was wrong. Dazed people were

plodding in his direction. They carried food, bundles of clothes, and precious bits such as altar gods or ancestors' swords. Behind them, smoke hovered over Kurikawa. Koji stood shocked until Spider jerked him off the road and they crashed into the bushes.

"That smoke's over Kurikawa!" Koji cried, struggling to pull away. "Let me go see—"

"No!" Spider squinted between the shrubs at the villagers.

Suddenly, Koji realized he wasn't a weakling anymore. He was a trained ninja. He drove an elbow into Spider's ribs and pulled free. He back-flipped away. Throwing down the pointy-shelled water chestnuts to hurt Spider's feet, he dashed across the dry autumn rice paddies toward home. Spider's shuriken sailed past his ear as he fled. By the time he reached the third field over from his own family's, Spider was panting on his neck. Koji snatched up a stick, spun around, and flung it at Spider's furious face. Spider lunged forward and knocked Koji to the ground.

"I have to go see what's wrong in Kurikawa!" he begged.

Spider hesitated, looking uncertain.

"I'm not running away! But I let my family down. I've been wishing . . . and dreading . . ." The look on Spider's face gave him hope, and he fell silent.

Spider turned from him to squint at a man some distance up the road. Wearing a fireman's many-layered coat, he rested against a thatched teahouse. His head lolled back and his mouth gaped open. He looked exhausted. "A fire," Spider said with rare sympathy in his voice. "All right, come on."

Careful to avoid people, they reached the edge of what had been Kurikawa. Now the village was nothing but clusters of burned debris, piled here and there where the thatched farmhouses had stood. The air was smoky. Spider's eyes looked red as he used his teeth to tear two pieces off his sash. He tied one piece around Koji's nose and mouth so he wouldn't breathe in the smoke, the other piece around his own face.

Shocked at the ashes fluttering in the breeze like dusty moths, Koji stumbled past the remains of the dumpling stand, then a kite maker's basket, overturned, with burned kites strewn on the ground. He stumbled into what had been his home. Now it was a burned wreck, all open, with a sooty breeze blowing around. What had been beams and the frames around paper shoji screens were now charred timbers and trash.

Koji felt as numb as a rock. He picked up a piece of the door frame Tanaka Shinzaemon had once knocked upon. Then he let it drop. His hands dangled, feeling almost detached.

His sluggish mind recalled the saying that in case of fire, if the ancestor tablets and deity statues were saved, things would turn out all right. But if either of these were destroyed, all was lost. He picked his way to the spot where the household altar had been and looked through the ashes.

"Koji."

He scooped up a handful of ashes and sifted

through them. He found a piece of the clay Buddha that had always stood beside his grandfather's memorial tablet on the altar.

Broken.

Something in his mind shattered. He began throwing around pieces of burned wood, all the time calling, "Mama, Papa, Taro. Mama, Papa, Taro. Mama . . ."

A sudden touch on his shoulder was a goad back to reality. His heart surged with hope and relief. His father had laid a hand on his shoulder that way so many times.

But when he spun around, it was only to face Spider. The torn piece of his sash covered his mouth and nose. "Come on, Koji. They're not here. Let's go home."

Koji pulled his shoulder out of Spider's grip. In a frenzy, he went on throwing around more half-burned objects and rubble. He picked up the large hook that had held the kettle suspended over the hearth fire for as long as he could remember. Attached to the hook was a wooden fish that could be moved to adjust the height of the pot. How many times had his mother warned him and Taro to stay back from the fire? "Friend Fish cannot prevent a burn if you're careless," she would say, waggling a fire tong at them as if she were shaking her finger. Koji cradled the fish in both hands. "Friend Fish," he moaned, rocking. "Friend Fish . . ."

Spider shook him. "Koji! *Koji!*"

Still gripping Friend Fish, Koji stared at Spider, unseeing.

Spider slapped him.

Koji dropped the wooden fish. When a shiver started deep, deep inside him, he hid his face in his sleeve and cried. The shivering wouldn't stop, and choking a little, he slid down onto the ground next to a piece of burned thatching. He couldn't get words past the hard lump in his throat and stared up at Spider through blurry tears.

The silence was like thunder.

Spider picked up his walking stick. "I'll go ask someone how the fire started. You won't—"

"No, I won't leave."

He sat stunned until Spider returned.

"Kurikawa couldn't pay Udo-sama's whole rice tax, so his samurai warriors burned the town."

Trying to take it in, Koji murmured, "That's why our mission took place last night and why so many castle guards were gone." Sharply, he looked up at Spider. "Your grandfather knew my village was being burned down."

"No, he didn't. When we know soldiers are leaving the castle, it's usually because spies have overheard conversations, seen them cleaning their swords and getting their horses ready. But that doesn't mean we always know what they're going to do."

Koji gazed at Crane Castle in the distance and at the ashes floating in the air between here and there. He remembered how proud he'd been, playing samurai warrior with cherry branch swords in the garden of the someru-ya. "I never thought Lord Udo would go this far," he managed to say. His heart could hardly believe it. But his head knew it was true, and in his gut a lump of hatred began to form.

"From this moment forward, I am a ninja," he said through clamped teeth.

"That word!" Spider warned.

With his jaw set, Koji made fists. "I want to be . . . grass. And I need to be grass." He reached into his kimono and touched his Jizo, carved by his father, prayed to with his brother, placed in his hands by his mother. His own words kept running through his mind: *I am a ninja . . . I am a ninja . . . I am a ninja. . . .* He squeezed Jizo hard.

Spider stepped around what had been the hearth, knelt next to Koji, and put his arm around his shoulders. "I used to have a father and little brother."

Koji blinked. The burnt house around him, so blurry through his tears, came into focus. "A brother like . . . me?"

Spider smiled. "A lot like you. My father and uncle took Shinbei on his first mission. Only Uncle Ox Tooth survived. He brought back my father's shinobi shozoku, but nothing of Shinbei's." Spider sat wrapping the end of his sash around his finger. "The night I captured you, I followed you for a long time before I attacked. When I realized you were lost, at first I decided that if you didn't come too close . . . But after all, I did have orders to kill trespassers. So finally I struck. Then I noticed the crane cloth and hesitated again. I thought it meant you came from the castle and would be helpful to us. I liked your spunk, and the cloth gave me an excuse not to harm you."

"I told you I wasn't from the castle."

"I know. When Grandfather met you, he realized you were telling the truth. An ordinary farm boy. You weren't much use to us, but he let you live. I guess he liked you."

Koji's shoulders sagged.

"Don't look so defeated. Don't you understand what I'm trying to say? You're right that you need to be grass. You've been brave since the first night, when you scrapped like a little tiger—and you so much smaller than me. Then I lit a smoke bomb in the cave and hid on a high ledge, remember? I watched you after you thought I had disappeared. Our methods already fascinated you." For a moment, Spider laid his arm across Koji's shoulders as if they were brothers. "I'm telling you that inside you've always been one of us."

A butterfly fluttered near Koji, colorful and unique among the drab ashes.

Spider glanced all around to be sure they were alone. "You were born with the heart of a ninja," he said softly.

Spider's words affected Koji all the more strongly because he had spoken the word "ninja" in the open. Koji stared at his Jizo as his heart pounded hard.

"I'm not used to talking this way." Spider pushed Koji back.

Koji sat running his fingertip over the one rough spot on Jizo's robe. "When you took me to the castle that day," he murmured, "I thought I was on a mission. But it was a trick. . . ."

"A test of your character, and you did well."

"No, I tried to run away. Dark Fire couldn't have gone on believing in me then," Koji said sadly.

"Remember, he never sees anything in absolute terms."

They sat with the smoke drifting around them. Koji looked around at the shell of his house. There was the spot where his parents had kept bowing to the master dye maker. There was the fish basket, partly burned, that Taro had taken to the riverbank. The kettle, on its side, had a puddle of soup in the bottom. *It's as if Mama saved my portion for me,* Koji thought. He felt as if his heart, in two pieces, lay at his feet.

"If my family was . . . dead . . . I would know it," he said suddenly. "I would know it, deep in my heart."

Spider didn't answer.

"Now that I've agreed to become grass, how can I do it without a ki bearer to impart its ki to me? That useless flute!"

"Why are you so sure I gave you the flute out of meanness?"

"Because—"

"Have you tried to learn to play it?"

"No." Koji scowled. "If I'm one of you, I deserve a weapon."

Spider sighed. "I dreamed about that flute, Koji, and you. If you knew what I dreamed, you'd guard it with your life."

"What did you dream?"

"Clear Mist told me I mustn't speak about it until ... well, I don't know until what. She said that I'll recognize the moment when I must reveal my dream. But I'll tell you this: once your ki is all wrapped up with a certain weapon, you can't find your life path without that weapon being part of your journey. So until you learn to play the flute, you won't be an effective fighter and—"

"No, I—" Koji began.

But Spider held up his hand to stop him. "Without the flute, you'll never find your family, either," he said gently. "Koji, for good or for bad, that flute is as much a part of you as your own skull."

Back in the ninja camp, Spider proudly carried the musket in the walking stick. He led Koji straight to Dark Fire, who was lying on cushions in the shade of a birch tree. The chunin was receiving his morning treatment for joint pain. The boys stood waiting while the camp masseuse placed pinches of powder on his back in four places. After lighting the powder with a stick of incense, she bowed and was gone.

Spider described their mission to Crane Castle and the fire. ". . . And Lord Udo's samurai warriors burned down Kurikawa. And you know Kurikawa is. . . was. . . Koji's village."

The powder on Dark Fire's back had burned away, and he sat up. "I knew from castle spies that something was going to take place last night," he murmured. "That's why many guards were gone. But I didn't know any details. I'm sorry, Koji."

Dark Fire's tone was so gentle that Koji bowed his head. He didn't want the old man to see his wet eyes. He remembered countless times when news rushed through the valley that Lord Udo's warriors were setting out to do battle with an enemy daimyo. He and Taro would race all the way to Crane Castle to see the men stream out on prancing horses.

The twins always hoped to arrive while the conch was still sounding the battle call. They would throw themselves down by the side of the road and admire the stallions with bright tassels on their bridles and around their necks, the spearmen in black lacquered armor and iron war hats. On the soldiers' backs, Udo-sama's scarlet banners flapped in the wind.

The sight had been breathtaking. But the memory of it now made Koji feel sick. "Sensei," he said, "I want . . . *need* . . . to do more to help you fight. Against evil."

Dark Fire's eyebrows rose in surprise.

"Because Udo-sama killed his family," Spider explained.

"No, they're not . . . ," Koji whispered. "They're alive. Somewhere." But where would they have gone?

"Leave us, Grandson," Dark Fire told Spider, wincing as he stretched his back.

Spider pulled the musket out of the walking stick. He gave it to Dark Fire, bowed, and strolled away.

"Beautiful," Dark Fire murmured, admiring the gun. Then he glanced up. "Koji, do you find yourself a ninja?" he asked, tapping his own chest over his heart. "Is that what I hear you saying? If your family—"

"My house was empty!" Koji shrilled. "My family is safe!"

"And a house is only paper and wood." A rare tenderness had crept into Dark Fire's voice. "Go meditate now on the pine that holds its greenery while other trees lose theirs."

Koji gazed at the musket. A bit of wood, a metal tube, and a clicker in the middle. A simple object, yet he remembered sensing its menace when he held it for the flat-faced samurai in Crane Castle. "Sensei, being a ninja requires four traits. Be strong. Know. Dare. Be silent."

"True. What is your point?"

"That weapon shoots firecrackers. They aren't silent."

"I see."

Koji wasn't sure how Dark Fire liked his comments, but he rushed on anyway. "The weapon is unsuitable to the ninja way. Also," he added, growing braver, "using swords, people can attack only those who are within arm's reach." He nodded at the musket. "That machine will cause more deaths than swords ever could."

"Wise words."

"Then we must break it."

Dark Fire handed Koji the musket.

The boy hauled the gun back over his shoulder. He cast an uncertain glance at Dark Fire. When the chunin gave a nod, Koji smashed the musket against a boulder. He banged it down again and again until it was ruined.

"From the beginning, I wanted it only to destroy it. Please bury it deep in the forest. But never tell anyone where."

Koji bowed low.

"Farm boy, by thinking like a ninja, you have this day saved many lives. At last, I am sure that my grandson did well to spare yours. In fact, I am certain enough to grant you a ninja name. From this day forward, you will be known as Blue Fingers. You have left that child, Koji, behind."

fter being renamed and burying the broken musket, Blue Fingers felt sure his life would improve. But after a few days, he realized that no simple name change could lift his troubles. Instead, resolved to find his family, he had no way to leave this mountain; resolved to be a ninja, he had no proper ki bearer.

When cold began creeping over the mountains, the ninja stuffed bark, pounded into coarse fibers, inside their clothes as insulation. But without a wadded cotton coat like the one he'd worn at home, Blue Fingers shivered.

"When it's cold, use your mind to turn yourself warm," Spider said. "And when it's hot, turn yourself cool."

"I don't know how," Blue Fingers snapped.

"No? Well, if you want to live in the ninja arsenal, you'd better learn to be tough. Come on, I'll teach you!" Spider added with a devilish grin. He dragged Blue Fingers up the mountain to the waterfall, roaring hard after a heavy rain. Spider grabbed him by both shoulders. Laughing, he thrust him under the icy waterfall. Squirming to get free, Blue Fingers gulped as the water pounded his hair flat.

"Don't you feel tougher already?" Spider shouted over the waterfall's roar.

Finally, Blue Fingers ripped himself out of Spider's grip. He collapsed, gasping, on the bank.

"Now think yourself warm," Spider called over his shoulder as he hiked away. "Any ninja can do it."

Blue Fingers couldn't, though, and soon he gave up wasting his time trying to think himself warm. Instead, whenever he found a moment alone, he would pray before the sakaki that grew near the ninja arsenal. "Kami-sama," he whispered to the tree's spirit, "I have a new name and I'm told that I am truly a ninja. But does being a ninja mean that I must live as a prisoner, never leaving this camp to search for my family?" He knelt, pulling at his lip, wondering if he dared ask Dark Fire or at least Spider whether he could now go in and out of camp like the other ninja.

He remembered what Spider had told him when they sat together in the remains of his house: that he would not find his family until he had woven that flute into his soul. Did Spider mean he wouldn't be allowed to leave camp until he could coax tunes from the thing? He didn't see how the flute and freedom could be related, but if they were . . .

Homesickness drove him to look for his abandoned flute among the scattered weapons in the ninja arsenal. Finally, buried under real weapons, he found the length of bamboo he despised. He drew it out, turned it in his hands, closed one eye, and peeped into the end. If only it concealed a blade or a secret chamber for explosive powders! But it was an ordinary bamboo flute.

He heard the chimes sound, telling him someone was entering the cave. He turned to look. Soon a folded camouflage cape, dyed to the forest's colors, slid in through the entrance. Falcon appeared a moment later, crawling along, pushing it from behind.

"I see you're finally learning to play your flute!" Falcon said, smiling.

Blue Fingers had forgotten he was holding his ki bearer and hid it behind his back.

Falcon's smile faded. "Don't be ashamed of it," he said, gently pulling on Blue Finger's arm. "I know how hard it is to adjust to this life. But you must at least accept that flute."

Blue Fingers grumbled under his breath.

"I understand. People like you and me . . . fitting in isn't easy."

Blue Fingers glanced up. "You and me?"

"Don't you know? I thought you'd figured it out. We're badgers from the same hole. I wasn't born into this life, either."

"What do you mean?"

"I also got lost in the forest and was found by the ninja."

"Like me?"

"It isn't unheard of."

"I did used to hear tales of a boy who vanished," Blue Fingers said, amazed. "You're not him, are you?"

Falcon laughed. "How can I know? By the time villagers were talking about my disappearance, I must have been gone. I don't even remember my parents' names. Although . . ." He gazed off for a moment before adding in a low tone, "Sometimes to put myself to sleep, I try to remember my home." He flashed a shy smile at Blue Fingers. "I don't recall which village or house I came from, but in my imagination I know every inch of the valley, every expression that crosses my mother's face. . . ."

"Sometimes I have trouble remembering, too."

"I suppose I'm only pretending," Falcon muttered, sweeping up grit from the cave floor, then flinging it down. "That's your world out there. Not mine."

"What was your name back then?"

"Who cares?" Falcon barked. "Toshio, I think." He set his jaw hard, then changed the subject. "Did Spider tell you about this flute?"

"He said he dreamed about it, but he wouldn't tell me what he dreamed. It's stupid and I hate it."

"Stupid? Didn't Spider tell you all he went through to get it? It doesn't only look like Udo Norimaru's flute. It *is* his flute."

"What!"

"For years, ever since Spider lost his father and brother, he's been obsessed with getting this flute. I was sick of hearing him go on about all the different plans he had to steal it. He finally managed to snatch it that time he took you to the castle to test your character."

"But why would he want a stupid flute? I don't."

Falcon hesitated. "Haven't you heard how Spider's father and brother were killed during a mission to Crane Castle?"

"What does the flute have to do with that?"

Falcon sat fidgeting with the end of his sash. "The mission went terribly wrong," he began, looking reluctant to speak. "Spider's father and brother were wounded. Some villagers saw the whole thing, and they told us about it later. Udo Norimaru happened by as they lay dying. Mind you, they were dressed as ordinary farmers, so he had no way of knowing they were ninja. But rather than help them, Norimaru sat down beside them and played that flute until they were dead. Once when Shinbei whimpered, he played a trill. Like a laugh, people said. Shinbei. Seven years old."

Blue Fingers stared at the flute in disbelief.

"It gets worse," Falcon went on. "Lord Udo loves to hear Norimaru's flute play, and he came to listen as they lay dying. He, too, simply stood by and let them perish. They were my friends. If you don't want the flute, can I have it?"

Blue Fingers tightened his hand around it, then

pressed it against his chest. "How can anyone stand by and let others die?"

Falcon nodded grimly. "Afterward, Spider kept dreaming that he knew how to play Norimaru's flute himself. He's been having that same dream over and over through the years since his father and brother died. I don't know why learning to play it felt like revenge to Spider. But it did. Once he finally stole the flute, though, he turned out to be hopeless at playing it. Then when he had that dream in which you were playing it, and playing it well, he was outraged!" Falcon threw back his head and laughed. "At first, he refused to do what the dream asked of him. But the dream kept coming back. Dream? Nightmare, to him, seeing you do what he couldn't! Mornings afterward, he was always grouchy. Don't you remember?"

"He always seems grouchy to me."

"Finally, he got Clear Mist's advice and gave the flute to you. Then the dream stopped." He held out his hand and asked again, "Since you don't want it, will you give it to me?"

Blue Fingers no longer wanted to be rid of the flute. "But it's my ki bearer," he said.

Falcon jerked back his hand. "Oh, I didn't know that! Then it's yours forever, whether you learn to play it or not."

Blue Fingers lifted it to his mouth and blew over the hole, but no sound came out. "I'm no better at it than Spider," he said, dismayed, "and it isn't even a weapon."

"Isn't it? Even words can be weapons." Falcon

stood up, brushing the silt from the cave floor off his clothes. "There's no going back on your ki bearer, Blue Fingers. Its selection is mystical. You think Spider picked it to provoke you? He wouldn't dare."

After Falcon had gone, Blue Fingers lifted the flute to his mouth again. He ballooned his cheeks and blew hard. When no tone came out, he pursed his lips and blew softly. Still nothing.

He gave up. He threw the flute down with the scattered weapons, then grabbed it and stuck it behind his sash instead.

Outside, snowflakes filled the leaden sky. Blue Fingers sniffed at them, discouraged. Had he really been here so long that soon snow would cover the world? Lord Udo had burned down Kurikawa after the rice harvest; with each passing moon, wasn't it less likely that he would ever find his family?

He went to Spider, who was alone, splitting bamboo on a stump. He was afraid to say what he must. But he plunged in by first announcing to Spider's back, "I'm a ninja now. I want to be. But I keep missing . . . well . . ."

Rhythmically, Spider lifted the ax over his shoulder, brought it down with a splintering crack, and lifted it again.

"And I am going to learn to play the flute now. Or try."

Spider didn't answer. He kept chopping bamboo.

Snowflakes drifted down on Blue Fingers's hair. He added in an uncertain tone, "Being a ninja can't mean

I will never know whether my family lived through that fire. That's too much to ask."

Spider hurled his ax blade into the stump. He swung around. "You don't decide what being a ninja means. And you don't decide what is and isn't too much to ask."

After a moment of shocked silence, Blue Fingers threw himself down on his knees. He pressed his forehead onto the frozen earth. "I want to find my family. Please!"

"Stand up," Spider hissed.

"I won't." Blue Fingers moaned into the dirt.

"I'm sick of you," Spider stormed. "Falcon and I used to be free. I'd rather drag a dead horse behind me than have you."

Blue Fingers felt as if Spider had spit in his face. "And I wish Falcon had found me," he said through his teeth. "Not you."

Spider reached down to slap Blue Fingers, but Blue Fingers knocked his hand away and sprang up. Spider tried to seize him by the collar, but Blue Fingers somersaulted away. He vaulted into a flying side kick and caught Spider on the shoulder.

It was the first time Blue Fingers stood a chance against Spider. He fought like a ninja, steady and determined. And Spider didn't win. The brawl petered out with Blue Fingers sliding his jaw left and right and Spider wiping his bloody nose.

"Tonight you take me down into the valley," Blue Fingers commanded. "As soon as I find my family, I'll come back. I promise! I'm a ninja, and ninja don't lie, and—"

"You must be simple-minded," Spider said, looking amazed. "You weren't born a ninja. Do you think Grandfather will let you dance in and out of camp? Certainly not alone!"

Suddenly, Blue Fingers's eyes felt strange, blind without being blind. He'd agreed to all they demanded, had even become a ninja. But still they refused to let him search for his family. It was what he'd feared, but hearing it declared out loud made it as final as the closing of a tomb. "But you said I've always had the heart of a ninja," he wailed.

"You'll have to prove to Grandfather that you're a ninja both inside camp and out."

"How can I prove a thing like that?"

Turning away, Spider laughed over his shoulder. "I don't know. But if I were you, I would learn how to play that flute."

B lue Fingers decided that if the path to finding his family lay in learning to play the flute, he would try hard. It took him days to coax a sound from it, but at last he did. He spent his free time practicing in the narrow passages that led from the ninja arsenal deep into the cavern-riddled mountain.

He'd never forgotten the song Udo Norimaru was playing when he stopped his sedan chair on the castle drawbridge. Now, as he remembered Norimaru with loathing, Blue Fingers practiced that tune, that and no other, again and again.

The melody sounded haunting within the strangely shaped passages. The notes echoed in one, had a ringing quality in another, and vibrated weirdly in a third. And somehow, as Blue Fingers's playing improved, he began to feel a little less helpless against the circumstances of his own life.

One winter morning, he even dared to practice up near the waterfall, where he knew some hidden ninja were guarding the camp. They were his first audience, whether they wished it or not. None of them came out of hiding to compliment him, but no one told him to keep quiet, either. And behind some snowy trees, a deer stood watching him, listening with its ears cocked.

By the time ice drenched the trees nearest the waterfall and turned them into a curtain of sparkling green glass, Blue Fingers knew he had mastered his first tune. Now he needed only to find the right moment to play for Dark Fire.

One freezing day at morning assembly, Dark Fire called Bear forward, then announced, "Last night Bear came upon three wolves together. They were surrounding a frightened woodcutter until singlehandedly, Bear slew them all. Good works of this magnitude have their own energy and power and must be rewarded." He lifted Bear's blowgun high and held it up in the air for several moments. Bear bowed to Dark Fire, then took the blowgun from him. He turned to the assemblage . . . they and Bear exchanged bows, he set off into the forest, carrying the blowgun.

"My uncle," Sky told Blue Fingers, beaming.

"What does it mean?"

"In this clan, when a ninja does a good work, especially for the poor people from the valley, Dark Fire offers his or her ki bearer up to Amida Buddha, and—"

"The ninja goes into the forest," Raven Wing went on eagerly. "He finds the perfect tree for—"

"One in which he senses its kami-sama?" Blue Fingers asked, remembering his first training session.

"Right. He feels a special sensation, too," said Sky.

"He places his weapon in a high elbow of the tree," Minnow added, looking up into some nearby branches.

Blue Fingers recalled the night when Spider had captured him. He had climbed a tree to look over the forest and, reaching up, gripped what looked and felt like the blade of a sword. "Over time, does the tree grow around the weapon?"

"Good guess!" Raven Wing said. "By putting his weapon into a tree, the ninja offers his ki to the spirit of the forest. When the tree grows around the weapon, it accepts it and merges with the spirit of the ninja who offered it."

"As the tree and weapon become one, the ninja's ki expands to blend with the ki of the forest," Minnow added. "When the forest's ki runs in a ninja's blood, he is remarkably powerful."

"Does every ninja eventually put his weapon in a tree?"

"Hardly!" Sky said. "My uncle Bear is the finest of the fine. All of us hope to be worthy to do it someday, though."

"The trees they choose aren't always near camp, are they?" Blue Fingers asked, still remembering his own adventure with the sword in the tree.

"Oh, no, some are quite far down the mountain," said Minnow. "Anywhere! The weapons in the trees serve a double purpose. If a trespasser came across something as strange as a part tree, part weapon, don't you think he'd turn back? It's one more way to protect our camp against intruders."

"No ninja could merge his ki with the forest's by playing a flute." Blue Fingers closed his mouth tightly so it wouldn't tremble.

That evening, Blue Fingers struggled to whittle a bird. On that faraway someday when he saw Taro, it would be nice to have a gift for him. But he eyed his creation in disgust, then flung it into the stream and watched it float away. It was nothing next to the things Taro could carve.

"Grandfather wants you, paddy frog," Spider said from behind.

Blue Fingers glanced across the clearing at Dark Fire, who looked angry as he talked to one of the training masters. "Am I in trouble?" he asked Spider.

"He's mad, but not at you. He's angry because . . . Did you think Lord Udo would say, 'Oh, well!' about losing that musket? He's furious and intends to get it back."

"But it's smashed."

"Then he'll try to get another one."

"We were fools to think breaking one musket would solve anything," Blue Fingers muttered. "We should have . . ." But his voice trailed off. He didn't know what they should have done.

He pushed past Spider and went to Dark Fire, and the old man led Blue Fingers aside to speak privately.

"I want you to do something for me, Blue Fingers. Something to help stop more muskets from coming into our valley. You see, before you brought me the gun, someone from this camp . . . I don't know who . . . met with Udo Norimaru and agreed to give him a diagram of it to be copied. That is an act of . . ." Dark Fire stared down at his clasped hands. "No," he murmured. "I will not label it 'betrayal' until I understand his or her motive."

He turned his glance to Blue Fingers. "The diagram I speak of is hidden in the cave near the waterfall. But if we seize it, whoever drew it will only make another. The person, not the drawing, must be dealt with."

"Whoever made it must have seen the musket. Who—"

Dark Fire cut him off. "Many ninja go on missions to Crane Castle and may have seen the musket. In fact, you're the only one who was unable to leave this camp while Udo-sama had the gun. Therefore, you are the only person who cannot have met with Udo Norimaru. This is why I chose you to help. Every other ninja is under suspicion. Even my own grandson," he added with a sigh.

"Spider wouldn't . . . ," Blue Fingers began. But he didn't finish. Was Spider cocky enough to try such a stunt simply to prove he could do it?

"I have reason to know that this person will retrieve the diagram after dark tonight," Dark Fire continued. "Go to the waterfall, hide, and watch the cave.

You know the one I mean. Simply tell me who you see, but don't mention this to anyone else."

At dusk, Blue Fingers made his way higher up the snowy mountain and slipped behind the ice curtain that the waterfall had formed by encasing nearby trees. At first, his heart raced with the excitement of the hunt. But as the winter forest darkened, he grew cold and bored. Maybe the traitor wasn't coming. Worse, what if someone did come and it was Spider? Blue Fingers wondered how he would ever look into Dark Fire's eyes and tell him his own grandson had double-crossed the clan.

Eventually, he heard footsteps in the underbrush, footsteps so quiet that no one but a ninja could have made them and no one but a ninja could have detected them. Moonlight flashed over a dark figure slipping into the cave, but from his angle, Blue Fingers couldn't make out who it was. He crept forward and crouched behind a boulder to peer directly at the gaping cave.

In time, the figure emerged, holding a bamboo tube, perfect for containing a rolled-up scroll.

Falcon.

As he slunk away through the trees, images of Falcon's many kindnesses flooded Blue Fingers's mind. *I don't want to get him in trouble,* he thought wildly. *But if I protect him, will Dark Fire find out anyway and punish me, too?* His chin dropped to his chest. He felt tired of being ninja Blue Fingers; he longed to be mischievous Koji again, a farm boy who knew nothing about weapons and strength and who had no trusted friend to betray.

But life snatched you by the throat whether you wished it or not, he thought, clenching his jaw. *And life named you Blue Fingers and flung you down here.*

He scurried down the mountain to cut Falcon off. He waited beside a certain woodland path, and when Falcon came into view, he stepped out onto the snowy trail to block the bigger boy's way. Falcon leaped back, jerking up his right hand. He gripped a walnut hull. Blue Fingers knew it must be filled with an explosive.

"Oh, it's only you," Falcon said, looking uncertain as he lowered his hand. "What are you doing here?"

"Catching you in the act of retrieving that," Blue Fingers said, nodding at the bamboo tube.

Falcon's face turned unfriendly, and he raised the walnut again. "I don't want to throw it," he warned. "But I will."

Blue Fingers faced the boy who had always taken his side. "Tell me this isn't what it seems," he said quietly. "Tell me it's one more test."

"Get out of my way, Koji."

"I'm the ninja Blue Fingers. Throw it if you dare."

Falcon hesitated. Then he dropped the walnut hull back into a pocket of his shinobi shozoku. "Koji . . . Blue Fingers . . . Your name doesn't matter. Call yourself anything, but leave me alone."

"Give me that," Blue Fingers said, holding out his hand.

"This?" Falcon's eyes were innocent as he shook a scroll of paper out of the tube. "You have the wrong idea. See?" He showed Blue Fingers both the front and back. The paper was blank.

"You forget I'm a ninja, too," Blue Fingers said. He took the scroll from Falcon and repeatedly licked it. As he did, the special ink, visible only when it was activated by saliva, began appearing on the empty paper. Soon a diagram of the musket had emerged. "How can you betray your own people this way, Falcon?"

Emotions flashed across Falcon's face: anger, desperation, shame. Then his eyes went cold. "I'm doing it because my name *does* matter. It matters that long ago I was Toshio, a farm boy. Now get out of my way."

"Why does being named Toshio mean you have to bring new weapons ... more death ... into our valley?"

Falcon raised his hand in a helpless gesture. "Udosama's son knows who my parents were. If I give him a diagram of the musket, he'll tell me about them."

"And reunite you with them?"

"Yes."

"No. He's a liar who's found your weak spot. I'm a villager, too, remember? When I was little, people talked about a boy who'd been lost. That must have been you. But Falcon, your parents were traveling through the valley. They stayed a long time, searching and hoping. But now they're long gone. I can't believe anyone knows where they are. Certainly the Udo family wouldn't know about people like them. Or care."

Falcon looked frantic. "I have to trust someone."

"You can trust Dark Fire. Did you tell Norimaru about us?"

Falcon looked startled. "That would be betrayal. I would never do that! Udo Norimaru thinks I've been a beggar since I lost my parents and that I glimpsed the weapon once when I was hanging around, hoping for scraps of food."

"Don't throw away your ninja family. They raised you."

Without looking up, Falcon murmured, "My mother's voice was the most beautiful sound I've ever heard. All I remember of her is her lullaby." A tear rolled down his cheek.

"I'm so sorry, Falcon. If you can sing the lullaby to me, I'll learn to play it for you on my flute."

Smiling sadly, Falcon held out his hand for the scroll. "Give it to me. I'm going to take it to Dark Fire myself."

Blue Fingers hesitated, but Falcon's steady, honest gaze made him hand over the scroll. "I'll go with you to explain."

"No, it's something I have to do alone. But if things are ever all right again, I *will* teach you Mama's song."

hen they reached the camp, Blue Fingers let Falcon go on ahead to where Dark Fire sat tending a night fire. Blue Fingers watched as Falcon threw himself down at the chunin's feet and as Dark Fire gently helped him up.

The two figures talked, silhouetted against the fire. Once Blue Fingers had reassured himself that Dark Fire wasn't calling guards to drag Falcon away, he turned to go. But from behind, Dark Fire called to him. Blue Fingers glanced over his shoulder to find the chunin hobbling nearer.

"Falcon told me what happened," the old man said. "I never understood the pain he has lived with because of losing his birth family. He will work on this issue and will not go in and out of camp until he has proved himself afresh." Tapping one fingernail against his walking stick, Dark Fire gazed at Blue

Fingers. "Falcon said you asked him if this was one more test. Why would I test you after honoring you with a ninja name?"

Blue Fingers looked away, feeling uncomfortable. "Because although you call me a ninja, you still don't let me leave this camp."

"You feel like a prisoner? But I didn't intend this to be one more test. Yet you did reveal your character."

Dark Fire smoothed his long beard as he appraised Blue Fingers. "Falcon is young and acted not from a traitorous heart but from homesickness. I would not wish to cast aside a trained ninja and young friend over what comes down to missing his mother. Intention matters to us, and you demonstrated that you understand our way without absolutes. You thought flexibly and showed mercy. Yet you also convinced Falcon to do the right thing. You handled the situation much as I would have myself."

"Sensei, now that we have the diagram, if Falcon promises not to make another one, is the issue of the musket finished?"

Dark Fire frowned. "Frankly, however Lord Udo obtained that first musket, he can use the same method to get another. Ultimately, we cannot stop muskets from coming into our valley."

"But you must have an idea," Blue Fingers said eagerly.

Dark Fire smiled sadly. "I do continue to meditate on this dilemma. Our hope lies in something subtle. Udo-sama is superstitious. . . . Perhaps we could trick him in a way that plays on those superstitions. But it takes time even for ninja to learn how to trigger such fears."

"And how to connect his superstition to getting more muskets," Blue Fingers agreed. Superstition . . . Blue Fingers recalled the many times he and Taro had denied being twins rather than see that frightened look in people's eyes. "Sensei, maybe I can help to trick Lord Udo. You see . . ." Blue Fingers clenched his fists for courage, then blurted, "I'm a twin."

For a moment, the chunin was motionless. Then his eyes rolled to look at Blue Fingers. "What did you say?"

"I said, I am a twin." Blue Fingers kept his voice level, but he couldn't stop twisting his hands. Had he said the wrong thing? So many people feared twins, and if Dark Fire felt that way, too . . . "You said 'superstition,' sensei. That made me think of my twin, Taro. Some people think twins are unlucky. But you'd like Taro. Everyone does. More than they like me. He does everything perfectly. He's strong and clever and careful. And brave."

"Hmm. I have heard of these beings called twins, but I have never met one. After all, whenever they are born . . ."

"Please don't be superstitious," Blue Fingers burst out.

"Superstitious? Ah, the villagers look at you that way?"

"Sometimes."

"But we ninja view many things differently from the villagers. People from your world fear doubles because they sense that the ki running between two born at once is uniquely powerful—supernaturally so. But while those in the valley fear the supernatural, we on the mountain honor it, embrace it, harness it for good. If you are a ki double, then my grandson was indeed wise to spare your life. Surely, Amida Buddha himself sent you to us." Dark Fire leaned closer. "So your twin is your exact image? But in every other way, he is your superior?"

"Yes, sensei."

"Then he must be a fine ninja. A better warrior than you."

"Well, no!" Blue Fingers said, stiffening. "Not that."

Dark Fire chuckled. But if he'd made a joke, Blue Fingers had missed it.

"Confronting Udo-sama with a set of ki doubles may indeed be our answer, although I don't know how." Then Dark Fire changed, barking orders at Blue Fingers. "Get my grandson. Tell him to take you down the mountain. This time he must show you the route back here. Give him these instructions: Leave you at the road to go find your ki double. Bring him to me."

"Tell my twin about this place? And all of you?"

Dark Fire hesitated. "If he is to help us in the ways possible by linking his ki with yours, then we have no choice but to trust him. However, after experiencing your ki, I know and trust you. Because of your mystical bond with your ki double, he must also be worthy of great trust."

"Should I confide in my parents, too? If I don't explain to them, they won't let either of us out of their sight—not after they already lost me once."

"They are the parents of ki doubles. This factor weighs in favor of granting them trust. But you are the only ninja who knows their characters. The decision as to what to tell them, and how, can only be yours."

Blue Fingers bowed and started to go. But from a few steps away, he glanced back at Dark Fire. "If I go into the valley alone, aren't you afraid I'll reveal the location of this camp?"

"You will remain silent about us. Now go. Hurry."

"But I have to know. Will I be silent because I will be a timid paddy frog all my life?"

"It is not for that reason that you will keep our secret."

"Then . . . ?"

"Blue Fingers," Dark Fire commanded, *"go!"*

lue Fingers dressed in the hemp clothes of a farm boy and finally set out to find Taro and his parents. For the first time, he made his way to Kurikawa without Spider at his side. As he went along, he strained his mind to think of how a set of twins could trick superstitious Lord Udo.

At last, he stood amid the rubble that had been his home. Pillows of wet snow lay on the charred timbers. Slush soaked his feet. But there was no sign that his family had visited the wrecked house since he'd been there with Spider.

Discouraged, he made his way to the village well. Normally, it was surrounded by women, chattering as they washed vegetables, rice, and clothes. But with Kurikawa destroyed, the well was deserted. Still, in time a stranger trudged to it from one of the few houses that had been rebuilt nearby. Backlit by the sunset, she came lugging a bucket in either hand.

Blue Fingers slid off the well. "Good evening, Auntie! Do you know where the people of Kurikawa are?"

She set down her buckets and, rubbing the small of her back, squinted at Blue Fingers. "Scattered or dead."

He closed his heart to her words. "Have you heard of a boy who suddenly disappeared without a trace?"

"The twin? Believe me, everyone knows that story," she said, puckering her lips in distaste. "He was stolen by tengu. Twins always bring bad luck. No wonder Kurikawa burned down."

Blue Fingers was shocked. Did their neighbors believe in some warped way that he and Taro had caused the fire? But he brought his attention back to what the woman was saying.

". . . and although he was a twin, the whole town searched for him. No use. If you're caught by tengu, that's the end of it."

Then he asked the question he had dreaded asking for months. "Do you know if the lost boy's family still lives?"

But she had finished filling her buckets and was turning away. "How should I know, boy?"

He'd left camp imagining a few minutes of asking questions, then by suppertime, a reunion with Mama, Papa, and Taro. At last, they would tell him they loved him despite his failure at the someru-ya. They would say it again and again.

Now he didn't know where else to seek them. He

plodded to the bamboo grove where Spider had brought him when they came down the mountain. Feeling gloomy, he dropped to the ground. He was starving, never had he felt so alone, and he had no idea what to do next.

He cleared the light snow from a spot of ground and pulled branches off pines. He tied the ends together, then fanned out the boughs and sat on them. Before leaving camp, he had rubbed oil on his body for warmth. It had been enough while he stayed active, but now he got out his iron pocket heater, lit a few coals in it, and huddled close. For supper he ate the only supplies he'd brought: tofu and plum syrup. Then he pulled more boughs over himself and slept.

He woke in the dark morning hours when the snow was dimly blue in the moonlight. To sharpen his night vision, he stared straight up into the purple sky as Spider had taught him to do. Suddenly, he had an idea whom he could ask for help finding his family. He struck out on the night road and ran all the way to the someru-ya. He circled the earthen wall, jumping to look over the top. Within, the garden was snowy, and more snow had drifted over the stone lantern and ornamental rocks in the Zen courtyard. Broom marks showed where the snow had been swept off the wooden walkway.

On the veranda of the house, freshly dyed strips of cloth, frozen stiff, hung from lacquered hangers. His foster family's geta stood lined up near the steps.

Obaasan's small shoes pointed in two directions as if reflecting their owner's obstinate nature.

He stuck his fingers through the locked wicker gate and shook it. When he couldn't open it, he wondered whether to shout and rouse the household. Now, they might wake up irritated. But Mama said he looked innocent when he slept. Wouldn't he touch their hearts if they found him tomorrow morning, sleeping in the snow? Or was he too changed, too strong for people to feel that way about him anymore?

Huddled shivering against the gate, he gazed up at the stars. How many times had he stared at them from the mountain camp? Were any ninja awake now and admiring the sky with him?

Those stars were like the eyes of sky kami-sama, all winking at him, telling him, yes, indeed, you're free at last. Free to seek your family, free to be Koji, free to be Blue Fingers, free to the marrow of your bones to be whoever you really are.

As his eyes started to close, he gave a contented sigh. *If only it's not Obaasan who happens upon me first . . .*

He woke, sputtering. Something was tugging him, and he found that Obaasan had him by the shoulders. Her expression, if not quite friendly, was at least less unfriendly than usual.

"That useless boy isn't dead. I found him! *I* did! Me!" she shouted as she dragged him up onto his feet.

Blue Fingers's foster parents were there within moments, their faces stunned.

"Look," Obaasan cried. She struck Blue Fingers with her bamboo-and-ivory pipe, but lightly and with a slight smile. "He's not even a ghost. He's alive."

"Udo-sama burned down my house," he said. "I'm searching for my family. . . ."

While he babbled on, the adults nodded. "Yes, we know about the fire, that you have a twin, everything. . . ."

"I'll search for my family forever," he declared at the end.

"Troublesome boy," Obaasan grumbled. "My parents died when I was your age." With unfocused eyes, she shuffled away.

"My parents aren't . . . ," he called to her retreating back. But he couldn't say that awful word.

"Of course they're not," Foster Mother soothed. Soon she was busy cooking. The delicious aromas of fish, vegetables, and steamed rice wafted to where the master dye maker and Blue Fingers sat talking. Blue Fingers was evasive about where he'd been. When his meal came, he held his rice bowl up to his mouth and, with ebony chopsticks, shoveled his food down too fast to talk.

The master dye maker told him how the villagers had searched for him the evening he disappeared. "She'll deny it, but the truth is that even Obaasan helped. She stayed at your house all night and kept miso soup simmering for when you arrived home."

"Obaasan?" Blue Fingers asked, disbelieving.

"While you were gone, we wondered how you

could have disappeared so absolutely." The man narrowed his eyes, thinking. "But as I see the skinny child I sent home, now looking so strong and capable, I have a theory about where you've been." The expression on the master dye maker's face made Blue Fingers nervous. But dropping the subject, the man instead finished, "Udo-sama is the villagers' enemy." His tone was calming, as if Blue Fingers were a bird that had to be caught. "He's my enemy, too."

"Yours! But you work for him."

"I work for him for the same reason your father pays his rice tax when he doesn't have enough food for his own family. What else can helpless people do?"

"You're not helpless."

"I am, compared to Udo-sama."

Blue Fingers had heard these ideas before, from both Spider and Dark Fire. But like a *tsunami* washing over him, now he understood. All that the ninja had told him was true.

"As soon as I finish with the dyeing wax, I will go try to learn anything I can about your family. We'll find them if . . ." The master dye maker didn't finish his sentence. "Have faith," he said instead.

Soon the master dye maker was ready to set out. "Stay here," he said, his face shaded by his conical straw hat.

"I want to go with you," Blue Fingers begged, holding his pleading hands up in front of his face.

The master dye maker put his hands around Blue Fingers's and lowered them. "If I go alone, people will answer my questions more honestly than with you at my side."

"If you go without me, I'll only run after you."

"Don't be the difficult puppy you were before. Remember what you've become." The master dye maker strode away, his footsteps crunching on the gravel path.

"What do you mean, 'what you've become'?" Blue Fingers called after him, but the master dye maker kept walking.

All morning, Blue Fingers worked over the dye pots. Later that afternoon, he went to the pond and, with one finger, traced the inscription "Good luck abides here" on the garden footbridge. Despite the snow, he could tell that fresh moss had sprouted in the characters he'd picked clean when he lived here.

It struck him that when he next saw his parents, it would be for the first time since he'd left for the someru-ya that stormy night. *I can't wait to find Mama and Papa, but what if they still don't want me and send me away again?* he wondered in confusion. *What if, all this time, they've been glad I was gone?*

He dragged his hand through the pond. He pushed water lilies this way and that, then looked up at the mountain. *My friends are up there,* he realized, *Falcon and Dark Fire and all of them. At least they want me—maybe even Spider does. And I still have to learn to play Falcon's mother's song for him.*

He noticed the master dye maker striding toward him from the house and scrambled to his feet. All day the boy had watched the gate for him. Yet somehow he had slipped by.

"No news," the man said. "But don't lose hope. Here and there, I left messages asking about your family."

Blue Fingers stood thinking as he smoothed the hem of his hemp jacket. The master dye maker was treating him differently—more as a grownup—than when he had been apprenticed here. *Am I acting differently myself?* he wondered. He had not run away when Obaasan spoke to him—even that small change was something new. He thought of the strange comments the master dye maker had made about him, "I have a theory about where you've been," and "Remember what you've become." Blue Fingers squared his shoulders; could the master dye maker have guessed that now he was a ninja? Hearing a sound, they both looked toward the someru-ya gate.

"Word travels fast," the dye maker murmured, for Blue Fingers's mother was coming in through the open gateway. When she saw her lost boy, she broke into a run.

The master dye maker left the reunited mother and son alone, and Blue Fingers and Mama both babbled at once.

"Where's Taro? Where's Papa?"

"Taro isn't far behind me." Mama embraced Blue Fingers, swaying a little. "Oh, Koji. My son! Where have you been?"

"On the mountain. Lost," he added, to cover the truth for the moment. "Is Papa coming with Taro?"

"But how did you survive?" she asked, then held him at arm's length and looked him up and down in amazement. "A child, lost in the wilderness . . . You should be like a skeleton! How did you grow so tall and strong, all alone out there?"

"I learned new skills. Please, what about Papa?"

"Don't ask me," Mama whispered, hardly moving her lips.

She wouldn't speak another word until she had bowed to her son's foster parents. Then she settled down on the tatami mat with Blue Fingers. "Son, your father is with his ancestors."

Blue Fingers stared. "No! I won't let you say that!" But he imagined what Dark Fire would say if he were here: "Ninja Blue Fingers, be strong. Dare. Be silent. And hardest of all, know." A ninja would not run away from the truth. "Tell me."

"He died defending Kurikawa from fire. He gave his own life to save many others." She made a resigned little gesture. "He couldn't have had a more honorable end."

Blue Fingers pictured his father wearing a fireman's outfit as he worked to put out the fire. He must have looked out through the hood's eye slits as if he were a ninja peering out of a zukin.

Then Taro arrived, running with his arms out to his brother. Blue Fingers leaped to his feet and ran, too. Taro had grown, and Blue Fingers saw him with new eyes. He didn't look like a better version of Koji—not anymore. And neither was Blue Fingers a flawed version of his twin. *Why, if you look closely enough, we're not even identical,* Blue Fingers realized in amazement. *Isn't Taro skinnier than me now? And he has that way of always biting on his lip. Besides, my leg is scarred where I cut it on thorns, and my arm is scarred where Spider cut me.*

The jumbled thoughts flashed through his mind in moments. Then Taro was upon him, and they hugged each other as hard as they could. As they hugged, Mama held one hand on each of their backs.

"Taro," Blue Fingers said, "I never noticed how fast you run! You could be a—"

"A what, Koji?"

Blue Fingers hesitated. But Dark Fire had authorized him to say what he must and, whispering, he plunged into a long explanation about where he'd been. All through his description, he watched Mama's and Taro's faces. He expected to see shock, dismay, horror. Instead, excitement blazed in Taro's face, and Mama smiled. "So you see, I have become one blade of grass," he said proudly. "And there are others, too. Some even lived in Kurikawa." He explained about the man who sold turtles and sparrows outside the temple.

"While some villagers have feared ninja, others have *been* ninja?" Mama asked. "I mean, have been grass? Yet we've always managed to live in harmony. Kurikawa has been like a person who ceaselessly stares at his own face in a mirror, never realizing that he has a back side, too.

"I know the man you mean, Koji. He is good." She gazed off for a moment, thinking. "If he is grass and fights against the evils that plague farmers, then you have my blessing to follow the same path."

Taking a step backward, Taro hung his head and began gnawing on his lip.

He won't be passed over again, Koji vowed silently as he reached out and pulled his brother forward. "My leader wants you to join our band, too, Taro," he said, and they both looked to Mama for her response.

Gently, she touched Taro's cheek, then Koji's. "You are my elder son, Koji, and now that your father is gone, you are the head of this family. You can make the decision to go live in the mountains, and if he wishes it, you may take your brother with you." Then she teased, "But don't think it means you can stop minding your mother—or visiting her in the valley!"

The twins and their mother knelt before the master dye maker's altar, graced with prayers written on small folded papers hanging from a straw rope. Mama had brought Papa's memorial tablet for her son to honor. She put it on the altar shelf, then Blue Fingers stood Jizo beside it amid the offerings of rice cakes, water, and salt.

He noticed the rough place on Jizo's robe. Suddenly, he knew why Papa had left that spot unfinished. Papa wanted his firstborn to contribute to the making of the cherished piece when the moment was right.

He asked Taro for the sheathed whittling knife he always kept tucked under his sash. While Mama and Taro watched, Blue Fingers made a few careful cuts and smoothed the jagged spot on Jizo's robe. Then he replaced it on the altar shelf beside Papa's memorial tablet. Gazing at the two side by side, an unfamiliar feeling of serenity settled over him like a cloak.

When they'd finished praying, they clapped and bowed. Then Taro showed Blue Fingers the wooden boat he'd carved for him.

"It survived the fire because I always had it with me, adding one last detail, then one more. I felt as if finishing it would jinx things so that you'd never come home! Oh, I missed you!" he cried, thrusting the boat at his brother. "And I'm sorry about what I said under the house. Was it my fault you left?"

"No, Taro. It wasn't like that."

"Anyway, I hope it looks more like a boat than an eggplant."

"It's beautiful," Blue Fingers murmured, stroking the boat with one finger. He felt a pang as he recalled the wooden bird he'd started carving for Taro, then tossed into the stream in frustration. "I wish I could make something for you, but . . . ," he began, then said instead, "Taro, I *do* have something to share with you. It's music. Later I'll show you what I mean."

"Taro, Koji looks so tired. Let him rest before Papa's memorial tablet," Mama said.

"There are carp in the pond, Taro," Blue Fingers said, still caressing the boat. "It's fun to lie on the footbridge and tickle them. I'll be right there, and we'll try floating this boat."

Taro leaped up, looking eager to investigate the pond. After he'd dashed away, Blue Fingers sat silently, aching for his father. One question had hollowed his heart, and a ninja must know. "Mama, I understand why you and Papa sent me here to the someru-ya in Taro's place."

"You do?" she asked, sounding so wary that dread crept through him. All his life, he'd suspected that his parents didn't love him as much as they loved Taro. But since that moment when they'd sent him away and kept Taro instead, he'd been sure.

Still, he'd expected Mama to deny it, to reassure him. When she didn't, he wanted to get up and walk away.

But he was a ninja, and a ninja dared.

"I wish you didn't know," she whispered. "Guilt weighed on your father and me every day of your life."

"Not *every* day?" Blue Fingers murmured, horrified. Surely she could look back on at least one day and know that they had both loved him then?

"Every moment," she said with certainty. "I wanted to tell you the truth. But your father couldn't bear to confess."

It was so much worse than Blue Fingers had imagined. Deep inside, he'd trusted that he would be proved wrong, that his parents would say, "Of course we love you! We always have."

"But . . . why couldn't you . . . love me?" he choked out.

Mama's shoulders jerked a little, she was so startled. "What is it you think, Koji?"

He couldn't look at her. "Papa sent me away because . . . you both sent me away because if you had to choose between us, you wanted Taro," he forced out. "Always Taro."

"Is that why you think we sent you to the someru-ya instead of him?" She covered her mouth with her fingers. "My poor child! We should have explained long ago. You see, Koji . . ." Anxiety had crept into her voice. "People believe twins are unlucky."

"I know. But we didn't bring you bad luck, did we?"

"Of course not. You two are my greatest joy. Your father's, too. You as much as Taro, and Taro as much as you."

Blue Fingers's heart gave a great, buoyant leap. "Truly?"

"Oh, Koji," she said, moaning. "There is more to it than that." She pressed her hand to her forehead. "Perhaps your father would warn me to keep the secret, even now. But I can't," she whispered. "We were so happy, knowing we would soon be parents. Being poor didn't matter, so long as we had a child to love.

"But having twins changed everything. We were afraid the neighbors would shun us. We'd heard stories like that. If the fishermen and tofu seller wouldn't sell us food and our neighbors wouldn't help harvest our rice, how would we live? How would we keep you two alive?" Her eyes darted around frantically. "So when two babies were born, we looked at both of you and . . . You were only a few hours old when we made the decision. It was the most difficult one of our lives."

"I don't understand," Blue Fingers said under his breath.

Mama's knuckles were white, as if her hands pushed out her words. "It could have been either one of you. But Taro was a bit bigger, a bit sturdier, a bit more active. He had a stronger cry, too. So your father tore a corner from the paper the fish was wrapped in. For our dinner. He wet it with his own saliva. He was careful, so gentle with you as . . . as . . ."

"What?"

"As he pressed that wet paper over your mouth and nose."

Blue Fingers stared at her in horror. "He . . . ?"

"Then we both turned away." She flashed a desperate glance at him. "We had to." Tears streamed down her face. "We turned our attention to the baby we later named Taro. We talked together. We were both careful not to glance in your direction." She paused. "And we counted the moments." Unlike that first day of his life when she'd looked away from him, now Mama stared into his eyes.

"After a minute, we were sure that . . . Well." She took both of her son's hands in her own. "So your father picked up that small bundle that was you, to take you to your ancestors."

Her eyelids fluttered. "Your father made a sound. In his throat. He tore the paper from your face and oh, Koji, you were still breathing! Somehow, unexplainably, you were alive. He hugged you and hugged you. He cried and stammered and . . . and I felt as if a butterfly had landed in my heart."

"Mama . . . ," Blue Fingers whispered.

She let go of Blue Fingers's hands. "We had done wrong," she admitted, looking away. "But it was the usual solution to such dilemmas. I know it's no excuse. . . ."

Blue Fingers couldn't speak.

"Forgive us."

"Yes," he managed. "But why did I live?"

"We wondered, too, so we consulted a fortune-teller. He said that Amida Buddha had not let you leave this incarnation because you had a great destiny to fulfill."

"Me? A great destiny?"

"Every day, as you grew up, we watched for signs of your unique future. The years came and went, but nothing unusual ever happened until that day when the master dye maker appeared at our door. How rare, for a fine man like him to offer an apprenticeship to a peasant. We realized that fate must have mixed up which of you boys should go. You were the one whose life had been spared at birth, you were supposed to be there at the riverbank, with Taro. And you are the one whom Amida Buddha has always held in the palm of his hand."

Mama, Blue Fingers, and Taro waved goodbye to the master dye maker's family. They set out as if for the hut Mama and Taro now shared in Aokusai. But once they were out of sight of the someru-ya, Blue Fingers and Taro left Mama. They went to the bamboo forest at the foot of the mountain. After Blue Fingers's mission was completed, either because he found his family or because he learned that they were forever gone, he was to wait for Spider here where they always stepped onto the road. Spider had agreed to look for him there each morning.

While the twins waited at the forest's edge, Blue Fingers began to teach Taro to leap, roll, throw, catch—one ninja trick after another. Excitement made Taro glow.

At dusk, they bent down a bamboo sapling and staked it to the ground. Over it, Blue Fingers spread branches to construct a shelter. He felled a pheasant with a shuriken, then raked together kindling and made a fire at the shelter's entrance. Besides enabling them to cook, it would keep out animals.

They roasted the game bird over the fire and, after soaking a gourd so it would not burn, used it as a pot to heat snow. They drank the warm water filtered through Blue Fingers's zukin.

"Look, Ko—Blue Fingers," Taro said, haphazardly flinging one of his brother's shuriken at a tall bush where some sparrows were perched for the night. When the shuriken hit the shrub, the birds all flew up and away.

Blue Fingers ran and picked up the shuriken. Gracefully, he spun around into perfect throwing stance. He glanced at Taro to see if he was impressed, but Taro looked defeated. His shoulders sagged. Blue Fingers was startled, and instead of throwing the shuriken, he went to Taro and pressed the blade into his hand.

"For you. It's your first weapon. You're going to be one terrific blade of grass, Taro. You'll leap, you'll flip, you'll fly!" Then Blue Fingers changed the subject. "Did you notice the direction the birds took when your shuriken hit the bush? I learned that when you flush out birds at rest, they always fly away from nearby settlements."

"Kurikawa and Aokusai are that way," Taro said, pointing as he analyzed the theory. "And the birds flew . . . You're right! I can't wait to learn more about being a—"

"Don't say it!" Blue Fingers cut him off, glancing around although they seemed to be alone. "Remember, we are grass."

Taro nodded. Then his smile faded, and sitting down, he flung away a twig. "You were so lucky, flying away from Kurikawa like those birds."

"Lucky!" Blue Fingers said as he settled down next to Taro. "I was guarded like a prisoner day and night. I missed all of you so much and couldn't even let you know I was alive. In the beginning, they acted as if they would kill me any minute!"

"But it was all worth it. Look, you're a . . . you're grass."

"And soon you'll be the same. But for you, the only pain will be in your muscles—not in your lonely heart."

"Yes, I'll become grass. Second," Taro said bitterly. "Second born, second to say my first word, and second ever after. That's why I've worked so hard to learn to whittle. To be first at something. Anything!"

Blue Fingers stared, speechless with disbelief.

"Even when I saved somebody's life, being a hero was taken away from me and given to you," Taro went on, his eyes glazed in thought. "The master dye maker welcomed you into his house. It was you who became his friend."

"But now . . . ," Blue Fingers began. His voice fell away as it struck him for the first time that he must find a way to tell the master dye maker the truth: that Taro had saved his life. *Why haven't I already thought to speak up and give Taro the credit?* he wondered, ashamed.

"Yes, now he knows me, too," Taro was saying. "But he met me through you. Second again. Because *your* destiny had to be attended to. Not mine."

Blue Fingers shook his head as if to clear his boggled mind.

Taro bit his lip. "I'm sorry. I try so hard not to care."

"It's not you who has things to be sorry for." Blue Fingers wanted to say more, but he was confused. The very air around them felt heavy and dead, and he couldn't bring out his thoughts. Still, he suddenly knew what ninja name he would someday give his brother. Great Hero. No. First Friend.

"Taro, I've felt second best, too. In other ways."

Taro gave him a doubtful sidelong glance.

"It's true! You do everything so well, even the way you whittle."

"Do you whittle, too?" Taro asked. He gestured toward the end of Blue Fingers's flute, stuck behind his sash. "That's a knife, right?"

"No, it's my flute." Blue Fingers remembered that he'd promised to share music with Taro. He pulled out the flute and showed Taro how to hold it. Like Blue Fingers before him, Taro couldn't draw out even one note. He turned it lengthwise and peered into it to see if anything was blocking the shaft. It almost looked as if he was sighting down the barrel of a gun, and Blue Fingers began to form an idea how to trick Lord Udo.

The next morning, Blue Fingers found Spider kneeling outside the shelter, waiting for them to awaken. Leaping up, Blue Fingers accidentally released the tied-down sapling that was the foundation of their shelter. It burst to pieces as he pulled on his sleeping brother's arm. "Taro, Taro!"

Taro sat up, rubbing his eyes. As he stared at Spider in his shinobi shozoku, a grin spread across his face. He glanced at Blue Fingers as if to say, "It's all true!"

Blue Fingers had expected Spider to ask many questions. Instead, he was already slipping away through the trees. "Don't you need to blindfold Taro?" Blue Fingers called to him.

Spider glanced back. "You're one of us, and he's your ki double. You decide whether we dare trust him."

"Of course we do," Blue Fingers said, smiling at the way his words caused Taro to straighten his spine.

"Then pay close attention to the route," Spider said as he stalked on. "And I mean both of you."

In camp, Blue Fingers crossed the clearing to Dark Fire. "I am back, sensei. This is my ki double, Taro."

The chunin smiled as he looked from one to the other. "You're like snowflakes . . . seemingly identical, but different enough that I can tell you apart. This pleases me greatly," he added. "Blue Fingers, show Taro around camp. You will be his teacher, as my grandson has been yours. Then rest. Lord Udo is already making plans to import more muskets into this valley, so we have no time to lose."

Taro flexed his hands. "Will we storm the castle? Me, too?"

"Ninja are ruled by four directives," said Dark Fire.

"A ninja is strong. He knows. He dares. And . . . ?" He glanced at Blue Fingers.

"A ninja is silent, sensei."

"Yes. That mandate leaves no room for open attack, Taro."

"But is there any other way to do battle?" Taro asked.

"You can chop down the biggest cryptomeria tree by repeatedly hacking away tiny chips. But leaning all your weight against a bamboo sapling doesn't take it down. No, we must formulate a different sort of plan. We are ninja, so our assault must be more ambiguous than open attack."

"I don't understand," Taro said.

"You will. For now, follow your ki double's lead. How can we stop Lord Udo from ever importing more muskets into the valley? That is the issue. We must think hard and fast, and if you are to be ready, Taro, you must train quickly."

"When will we strike, sensei?" Blue Fingers asked.

"Lord Udo pretends he is the most powerful man in Japan, but he is not," Dark Fire said. "That position goes to the shogun."

"Yes, you once told me that," Blue Fingers said. "But—"

Dark Fire held up his hand for silence. "The shogun has commanded Udo-sama to come to Edo and explain why he burned down his own village. Lord Udo should leave within a few weeks."

"How can we even approach him if he isn't here?" Taro asked.

"Boys, think like ninja. I said that Lord Udo *should* leave within a few weeks. Predicting behavior begins with analyzing character. If the shogun has commanded Lord Udo to justify himself . . ."

"He is arrogant and will refuse," Blue Fingers said.

"Yes. Please take your prediction a step further."

"Will he send someone in his place?" Blue Fingers asked. "Someone intimidating."

"His whole army?" Taro asked uncertainly. "Or most of it?"

"Good thinking, boys. We will strike when only the bare bones of the army is here to guard Crane Castle."

"I've been thinking," Blue Fingers said. He looked down at his flute, remembering when Taro held it turned lengthwise, as if he were aiming the musket. "Couldn't we use Norimaru's flute to prey on his father's superstitious mind?"

"Please tell me more."

"Well, if Lord Udo heard Norimaru's tune playing, but Norimaru wasn't there . . . I mean, if I was playing Norimaru's special tune, but I was hidden so that the sound seemed to come out of nowhere, and . . . and . . . and the musket will somehow relate to the tune, so Lord Udo thinks Norimaru and the musket are connected, and maybe he'll be superstitious and . . ." Blue Fingers fell silent for a few moments. "I guess it's just the beginning of an idea," he admitted. "I haven't worked out the details."

Blue Fingers hadn't noticed Spider nearby, listening,

but now he came closer. "Maybe we can work out the details together," he said. "You see, I had a strange dream about what you're describing. That's how I knew the flute was meant to be your ki bearer. The moment has come for me to share my dream."

As Spider described his dream, Dark Fire rubbed his hands together eagerly. "You boys will begin this trick on the night when the army marches out of Crane Castle and starts toward Edo. Taro, we will need your help, too," he said, appraising Blue Finger's thinner, weaker twin.

"But I'm not a ninja," Taro said, biting his lower lip.

"Not yet. But your role in this mission will be uncomplicated, and I trust that you are strong and determined, like your ki double. If you train hard between now and when we need your help—perhaps harder than any ninja has ever trained before—you can be ready. And please do not confuse uncomplicated with unimportant. You will become a ninja, and today is not too soon for you to start your new life."

Taro bowed to Dark Fire. "I will do all you ask and do my best. I hope I can make you as proud as Ko—Blue Fingers has."

Dark Fire smiled, then clapped once. "Let us play a ninja trick on Lord Udo."

Never before had Blue Fingers seen Dark Fire's eyes twinkle. But they twinkled now.

ntil the army left the castle a few weeks later, Blue Fingers saw little of Taro, who was training hard. Completion of the ninja trick would require three nights' work. On the first night of the mission, Blue Fingers showed Taro the white shinobi shozuku he and Spider would be wearing to blend in with the snow.

"Do you truly feel ready to go on a mission by yourself?" Dark Fire asked Blue Fingers. "My grandson will stay in the castle only long enough to show you the place where you must perform your assignment."

"I know I'm ready."

"Be careful!" Taro reminded him and Spider as they set out.

Under a moon as slim as a willow whip, Blue Fingers and Spider crept down the winter mountain.

They each wore pieces of sharpened bamboo attached horizontally to the soles of their feet. These prevented them from slipping on ice and, instead of footprints, left puzzling parallel lines. Over his shoulder, Blue Fingers lugged a sack . . . a sack full of lumps that moved.

Once they had snuck onto the grounds of Crane Castle, they removed the bamboo from their feet. They replaced the bamboo with metal spikes, and put spiked leather bands on their hands. Along with grappling hooks, spiked feet and hands helped them climb the walls to the parapet outside Lord Udo's winter bed-chamber.

The wind whipped hard on the parapet as Blue Fingers stood watch for guards. Nearby, Spider crouched to work at a certain stone in the wall. At last he pulled it from the spot where it was wedged between others. It hid a space under the floorboards that was too narrow for Spider. "You're on your own," he whispered to Blue Fingers. "Good luck."

"Have you forgotten something?" Blue Fingers asked as Spider turned to go.

"Shh! Forgotten what?"

"Poisoned pellet," Blue Fingers whispered.

"I know you. You won't be caught." He set off for the bamboo tree where Blue Fingers had crossed the castle wall. When Blue Fingers heard a hototogisu bird from that direction, he knew that Spider was safely outside the castle.

On his belly and pushing the lumpy bag ahead of

him, Blue Fingers slipped into the opening. He moved slowly, sliding his open hand over the floor in front of him, feeling for a gouge a previous ninja had made. When he finally touched it, he knew he was directly under Lord Udo's sleep chamber.

Blue Fingers reached around to the front of the bag and managed to empty its contents: fifteen sluggish wood frogs that had been hibernating in the ninja camp's animal cave. In the relative warmth inside the castle, the frogs would awaken, and their croaking would disturb Udo-sama's sleep.

The ninja had performed the trick before, and it always worked the same way. The frogs' croaking kept Lord Udo awake, so that he grew overtired and irritable. Soon others began keeping their distance from him. The slight restraint in Lord Udo's few sentries would give the ninja their chance to move in close to him and attack.

Best of all, the ninja had released frogs below the castle floor enough times before that to those who lived within Crane Castle, frogs had become a source of superstition. The people believed that when frogs became plentiful around the castle, something bad was sure to happen. Now, more than ever, Lord Udo's superstitions would be strong.

Once the bag was empty of frogs, Blue Fingers waited. He was more cramped here than in the tunnel to the moat. But now he was trained to control his panic by focusing on his breathing. He listened to the frogs as they awoke, one after another, and began croaking.

"Not this again! Silence them!" Lord Udo commanded. After a mumbled answer from someone, he roared, "One frog? There must be a hundred! How do they find their way here? Especially at this time of year. I told you last time that it'd better never happen again. Catch those frogs now or pay with your neck!"

Another murmured answer, this time tinged with fear.

Blue Fingers waited until silence—except for the croaking frogs—indicated that Lord Udo was alone. Then the young ninja fitted his flute to his mouth. Quietly, he played only the middle strain of Norimaru's tune, starting and ending softly, to give the illusion that the sound came out of nowhere and returned there. He paused, then played the same bit again and again. Only when he heard Lord Udo ask doubtfully, almost fearfully, "Norimaru . . . son . . . ? Are you there?" did he know he had done a good night's work.

He backed out of the space below the floorboards and at the tenshu wall pushed himself out from underneath the floor. Dawn had come. He knew he must hurry, but he couldn't help pausing for a moment to smile up at the sky. "Lord Amida Buddha," he whispered, "do you see what I've done? My first real mission, with no one watching over me. They trust me!"

Spider was waiting in the bamboo grove beside the road. "Do you know your way to camp now, Blue Fingers? Can you lead?"

"Aren't you going to ask me if I completed my mission?"

"Didn't I train you myself?" Spider asked. "If I don't have faith in you, who will?" Then, as if to remind Blue Fingers who was boss, Spider shoved him hard. "Hurry up, lead us home."

With Spider correcting him when he wandered in the wrong direction, Blue Fingers found his way to the mountain camp. But after only a few hours of exhausted sleep, it was time for another day.

The second night's mission was like the first, except that Blue Fingers was alone from the beginning. He set out from camp when he felt it was dark enough and without anyone even saying goodbye. This was entirely his own operation.

He crept down the mountain and, as he had the night before, waited in silence under the floorboards. He remembered a conversation Dark Fire had told him about. Lord Udo's daughter had, as expected, told Jade Bat—O Kei—of the strange way her father had heard Norimaru playing his flute in the night.

"But O Kei," she had mused, combing her long hair, "Norimaru was asleep in his own chamber at that time. What can it mean?"

"Perhaps it was a message from Amida Buddha," O Kei said.

Alarmed, the girl looked around. "What kind of message?"

"Pray that tonight Amida Buddha tells your father more. If he hears Norimaru's tune two nights in a row, surely your brother is in grave danger."

When the moment was right, Blue Fingers fitted

his flute to his lips. He played Norimaru's tune over the croaking of frogs, as he had the night before. But this time, Lord Udo neither shouted nor raved.

Blue Fingers's heart hammered with excitement. *Lord Udo is listening,* he thought. *He's trying to figure it all out.*

He longed to go into Lord Udo's sleep chamber and complete the trick right now. But although it had never been named as a ninja directive, he knew that an unspoken fifth was patience. So after playing the middle phrase of Norimaru's tune three times, he backed out from under Lord Udo's sleep chamber and went home.

The very next night, they would play the ultimate ninja trick on Lord Udo.

n the third night, Blue Fingers, Spider, and Taro went down the mountain to finish the trick. Before they started, Spider looked Blue Fingers up and down. "I want to ask if you're sure you can do this, but you know what? I know you can."

"Are you saying that you trust me . . . as a ninja?"

"Would I put my life in your hands if I didn't? I warned you that change comes slowly, but it does happen eventually. Good luck, O favorite pupil of mine." With genuine fondness in his eyes, Spider flashed Blue Fingers a grin.

"*Only* pupil of yours," Blue Fingers corrected, smiling, too.

The boys hiked down the mountain wearing winter shinobi shozoku. Spider carried a dead fox. Taro had a piece of wood carved to look like the musket. Blue Fingers carried a piece of cloth saturated with Norimaru's camellia flower scent, and each boy had a costume tied in a bundle on his shoulder. They slipped onto the lightly guarded castle grounds and up the castle wall to the parapet.

Hidden within shadows, they went to Lord Udo's window. They tied lacquered cloths around their mouths and noses, then Spider lit an incenselike sleeping potion. He waved his hand through the air to drive the smoke toward the nearest guard. Eventually, the man's head nodded and the boys slunk along the wall to him and eased him to the floor.

Outside Udo-sama's window, they changed into their costumes. The twins put on matching kimono. Spider wore an elaborate kamishimo identical to one of Norimaru's: pale blue starched hakama and a samurai's winged jacket. A flute was tucked behind his sash.

Spider crept to Udo-sama's room, with the twins following. He slid the slatted window open enough for them to peek into the room. Within, a nearby candle lit the corner where they must enter. Spider frowned, thinking. "A candle. No. Too bright," he whispered. "If Lord Udo wakes up . . . Go back."

Blue Fingers was puzzled. "When you stole the musket, Spider, his room was much darker."

"Shh! Your flute must have spooked him, so he keeps a candle lit. Turn around, we have to give up."

"But—"

"No more talk."

As Blue Fingers swung around to go, he noticed a

pad of snow on the outside of the window, near Taro's elbow. Blue Fingers reached past his twin and swept it up. With his free hand, he pushed the window open wider. Then he flung the snow at the candle.

With a ninja's unerring aim, he snuffed it. He was pleased to see the surprised look on Spider's face before he slipped through the window into the dark room.

Once inside, Blue Fingers dropped the perfumed cloth into the liquid wax pooled in the candle. Mingled with the hot wax, Norimaru's camellia scent wafted out into the room as Lord Udo slept.

Next, Spider tossed an obi out over the tatami mats that covered the floor; their footsteps would be quieter on cloth than straw. He stole across the room to the alcove where they would perform the trick. There, he drove a dagger into the belly of the dead fox he'd brought down the mountain. He let its blood drip onto the floor. Then he tossed the carcass to Blue Fingers, who dropped it into a shadowed corner outside the window. They would retrieve it when they slunk away.

As Lord Udo slept on, the twins slipped behind one pillar, Spider behind another. Quietly, Blue Fingers played Norimaru's tune again . . . and again . . . and again. . . .

He played for a long time before Lord Udo awakened. When he did, the samurai muttered, "That tune . . . that tune . . . How I used to love it, but now it will drive me mad!"

As Blue Fingers played on, Spider stepped out from behind a pillar just far enough for Lord Udo to notice him. Then he immediately stepped back.

Lord Udo stiffened. He rubbed his eyes. "Son?" he called into the darkness as Norimaru's tune began yet again. He sniffed at the air. "I hear you and smell you and see you. But your flute is stuck into your sash, so how can you be playing it?"

As Blue Fingers went on repeating Norimaru's tune, Lord Udo pulled the quilt up to his chin, licked his finger, and wet his eyebrows to ward off tengu.

Together, Taro and Blue Fingers stepped out from behind their pillar. Standing directly behind Taro, Blue Fingers was hidden from Lord Udo's view. He went on playing his flute while Taro held the wooden musket horizontally with the stock against his cheek so it hid Blue Fingers's flute. It was as if Norimaru's tune emerged from the gun. While Blue Fingers kept playing, he and Taro moved apart to make Lord Udo think he was seeing double. But one image played music on a flute, the other on a gun.

Dressed as Norimaru and mimicking his arrogant walk, Spider appeared again from behind the second pillar. As he strode directly in front of the gun Taro held, Blue Fingers stopped playing the flute and stepped out of sight.

The sudden silence intensified the weird atmosphere as Taro turned the musket. He aimed it at Spider when he stood over the bloody spot on the floor.

At the same moment, Blue Fingers reached into

the front pocket of his kimono for a smoke bomb made from blood, urine, ashes, sulfur, charcoal, and nettles. He lit it and flung it down. It hit the floor with a bang.

When the smoke bomb exploded, Spider/Norimaru collapsed as if he'd been shot by a gun playing his own tune.

As Taro melted into the shadows, Lord Udo scrambled out of bed. "Guard!" he screamed while smoke fanned out into the alcove. Shielded by it, Spider crawled behind a pillar to hide.

The smoke was still thick as Lord Udo ran to the door and slid it aside. "Bring the oracle to interpret my dream!" he shouted into the corridor. While he was distracted, the three boys slipped out the window, Blue Fingers snatching the camellia-scented cloth as he went.

With a teasing grin, Spider elbowed him in the ribs. "You carry that bloody fox."

"The newest ninja does the messy work?" Blue Fingers joked. He was smiling, too.

With Taro and Spider, Blue Fingers crawled into the ninja arsenal and dropped into an exhausted sleep. It seemed only a moment later that Dark Fire's voice was urgently awakening him. Too big to enter the arsenal, he was calling from outside the entryway.

Blue Fingers crawled through the shaft. "Sensei, what's wrong?" he asked anxiously. "Did our mission fail?"

"Calm yourself. I am coming to tell you how well it went. Jade Bat has sent word. Thanks to you, Taro, and my grandson, our superstitious Lord Udo thinks he has had a prophetic dream. The real blood on the floor has confused and convinced even his most skeptical advisers. They all believe that importing guns into this valley will lead to Norimaru's death. Udo-sama is preparing to send a messenger to cancel the order for a shipment of muskets. So! My grandson is already at the morning assembly, but please wake Taro and come."

The twins arrived at the training grounds and started toward the spot where their age group stood.

But Dark Fire held them back. "Something has happened that requires an unusual response. Please remain here in front. Grandson," he called, "you come forward, too."

When all three boys stood beside him, Dark Fire asked them, "How do you evaluate last night's mission?"

The three exchanged uncertain glances. Then Blue Fingers spoke for all of them. "We thought it went all right."

"Indeed, it was highly successful. I suspected, though, that you did not comprehend the importance of what you did. Then let me clarify the matter. The worst fate that can befall a ninja is for his identity to be revealed. Therefore, only rarely does a ninja . . . a truly brave one . . . intentionally confront his enemy face-to-face. Yet last night, all three of you did that."

Blue Fingers stared at the chunin, amazed that their modest assignment could evoke this speech.

"And as to you, Blue Fingers, no one knows better than ninja that even slight uneasiness upsets one's breathing. During moments of stress, some people find themselves holding their breath. Others pant. Few breathe normally. But during the whole time you faced Lord Udo, you continued breathing calmly enough to play the flute. Rare courage."

"Breathing isn't courageous!" Blue Fingers said.

"Oh, but it is. Breathing reveals what is going on inside a person." He paused, studying Blue Fingers's expression; then he added, "If you don't believe me when I tell you that you acted courageously, look at your fellow ninja's faces."

Still embarrassed, Blue Fingers stole a glance at the faces before him. He couldn't believe their expressions. All the ninja looked impressed, even Sky, Minnow, and especially Raven Wing. In unison, all the assembled ninja bowed to the three boys.

Blue Fingers reached into the front pocket of his kimono and felt the sharp point of one of his shuriken. The little blades would always be important to him. But he gripped his flute tightly. The day would never arrive when he willingly changed to a different ki bearer. Not even shuriken. *One day,* he decided, *I will complete a mission important enough to place my ki bearer in a tree. And that ki bearer will be my flute.*

The three boys bowed first to Dark Fire, then to all the ninja assembled there. They bowed to each other, too. As Blue Fingers faced his twin, he smiled to see how proud Taro looked. *Of the three of us, he has the most to be proud of,* Blue Fingers thought. *This mission was important, but saving someone's life is bigger.*

"You'll really teach me all you know about ninjutsu?" Taro asked him, twisting his hands anxiously after the assembly broke up. "I can't wait to become more like you," he added, ducking his head shyly.

"Become more like me? Taro, you're the hero." But seeing Taro's bony arm beside his own muscular one, Blue Fingers understood things from his twin's viewpoint. Taro had saved the master dye maker's life, that much was true. But his heroism had come to nothing. No one but the twins and Mama even knew what Taro had done. *The master dye maker himself still believes I'm the hero,* Blue Fingers thought, realizing how unfair that was. *I can't let this misunderstanding go on any longer.*

"I have to go into the valley," he told Taro abruptly.

"But . . ."

"I have unfinished business and I have to go now." He pivoted and plunged into the forest and down the mountain, still hardly believing that he could wander away freely.

As he slipped in through the gate to the someru-ya, he felt self-assured. But when the master dye maker stepped out onto the veranda to meet him, Blue Fingers's confidence wavered. He felt like that naughty little boy who had pulled up peonies and had plucked all the moss from the chiseled inscription on the foot-bridge.

The master dye maker put both big fists on his hips. All he said was, "So."

Blue Fingers paused, steadying his nerves. "I have come to tell you something important."

The master dye maker held up one hand to stop Blue Fingers from speaking. "I have important information for you, too. But it is not so easily put into words."

For a long time, the master dye maker remained

silent, stroking his chin. "Do you have a new name?" he finally asked.

Blue Fingers stared in astonishment. A new name . . . Could he possibly mean a ninja name?

He seemed about to say more, then turned away instead. "Come. I have things to show you."

he master dye maker showed Blue Fingers the four steps that led to the dye shop's raised back wing. Then, to the boy's astonishment, he slid the whole staircase aside in one piece. The area behind the stairs formed a small hidden room, the front side of it consisting of the sliding steps.

"Do you understand?" the master dye maker asked.

"It looks like . . . ," Blue Fingers began. But he couldn't force out his idea.

"Yes. It's a hiding place for . . ." The man stopped short, then glanced around cautiously. ". . . blades of grass."

Blue Fingers stood paralyzed as the master dye maker's words rang in his ears.

"Notice that the steps' risers are made of paper. Someone stationed in this cubbyhole can hear everything going on out here where we are. Should an enemy climb the stairs, hidden grass could thrust a sword through the paper and cut him down." The man gripped Blue Fingers's arm and propelled him onward through the house and shop. Blue Fingers had seen it all before, but now he saw it through fresh eyes. The buildings were filled with a maze of secret passageways and trick doors. What looked like an ordinary scroll painting concealed the entrance to a sort of cupboard where one could hide. Hallways ended in traps. Removable floorboards hid swords. Flower arrangements camouflaged knives. Incense sticks were ready to be lit, not to release fragrance, but sleeping potions.

Overhead, a low ceiling screened a higher one. A sword thrust up in search of concealed ninja would find emptiness while the ninja, lurking higher, remained unharmed. And the sandy courtyard surrounding the house was an alarm. Few people would be skilled enough to cross it silently, and none without leaving footprints.

In one room, the master dye maker carefully positioned Blue Fingers beside him in the corner. He kicked his heel back against the wall. Though the floor under them remained stable, the rest of the floor tilted. Someone standing elsewhere in the room would have been tipped into the cellar, lined with bamboo spikes.

The master dye maker slid aside the false bottom of a broad vase to reveal an escape tunnel.

"May I . . . ?" Blue Fingers asked, and lowered himself into the shaft. It was snug around his shoulders, and he squatted there, trying to take it all in. Overhead, the master dye maker was a looming shape. If Blue Fingers didn't know him, his very size would have been frightening. *Something about him is threatening,* the boy realized. *Funny how I trust him anyway.*

Ambiguity.

Blue Fingers gasped as if he'd been pushed outside into the snow. *Could this man be our jonin,* he wondered.

As Blue Fingers glanced up, a glimmer of understanding flashed in the master dye maker's eyes. But before Blue Fingers spoke, he saw warning in the sharp glance.

Ever so slightly, Blue Fingers nodded. He would never speak of what he had guessed.

He climbed out of the tunnel and replaced the vase on top of it. For a moment, he stood facing the only other blue-fingered person he'd ever met. Then the master dye maker turned and walked out of the room. Blue Fingers shuffled his feet a little; he didn't know whether he was supposed to follow or stay.

But after a moment, the man returned. He drew his hands out from behind his back. "We have something for you," he said, holding out to Blue Fingers a packet of folded cloth wrapped in rice paper. "It's from all of us." He gestured toward Foster Mother and Obaasan, both peeking at them from an open doorway.

Blue Fingers pulled away the paper and shook out the cloth inside. His jaw dropped. It was a shinobi shozoku just his size.

"Your foster mother and Obaasan sewed this for you."

Dumbfounded, Blue Fingers hugged the cloth. It was the most precious thing he had ever owned. "Thank you!" Blue Fingers said, bowing to the master dye maker, then to Foster Mother and Obaasan. They bowed back, beaming, before disappearing from the doorway.

"Koji—"

"My new name is Blue Fingers."

The master dye maker smiled broadly. "Blue Fingers, I have no son . . . no heir to inherit my work. I've always worried about that. When the boy I finally chose seemed so ill suited for my work, I thought that my grandfather's carved good-luck charm had let me down at last." He gazed in the direction of the inscribed stone footbridge in the garden, then back at Blue Fingers. "Now I find myself looking at you differently and feel the need to ask again. Would you like to follow in my footsteps?"

"Your work . . . You mean inherit the dye shop? Or . . ." Blue Fingers fell silent.

"I see," the master dye maker murmured, disappointed.

"No, you don't. I want to accept with all my heart. But once you know the truth, you won't want me." Blue Fingers's throat felt locked in pain, but somehow he forced out the words, "I have to confess. I never saved your life. It was Taro."

If the boy had not been staring at the man's broad

feet during the long silence that followed, he would have thought the man had walked away.

"I realized that as soon as I met him," the master dye maker finally said quietly. "He has a mannerism— he bites on his lower lip when he's stressed. The moment I saw him do it, the image rushed back to me of him standing on the riverbank, holding old Ryoshi's pole out to me. He was chewing so hard on his lip that I'm surprised it didn't bleed. Then when I noticed that whittling knife he keeps tucked under his sash . . . I remembered that the pole was tangled in a fishnet. The boy who saved me had a knife right at hand. Without it, he couldn't have untangled the pole fast enough to save me." His gaze held Blue Fingers's steadily as he waited to hear what the boy would say.

"Then you understand. Taro is your hero—not me. And I can't take an opportunity that should be his. Not again. You should make your offer to him."

"Taro has much to be proud of, but the fact that you've set the record straight impresses me. You are the one I have chosen, and if you agree, my choice stands. The universe has its own timing, and Taro's moment will come. I shall make sure of that. But this moment is yours."

Blue Fingers shifted from foot to foot. "Truly?" he whispered, and something in the way the master dye maker lifted one eyebrow told him *yes*. Blue Fingers squeezed his hands into fists. "Then—yes! If you're sure! You must know about everything. Ki bearers and—"

Frowning, the master dye maker crossed his arms

for silence. "I wanted you to know what the other blades of grass know, that I run a safe house where they can rest. But I don't know where the camp is. Don't tell me anything. Especially not names."

"Does Foster Mother know?"

"She and Obaasan are also friends to those who are grass. You're very young, and when I admit that this is a safe house, I hope you understand the trust I'm putting into your hands."

Blue Fingers bowed. "Foster Father," he said, addressing the master dye maker that way for the first time since he had run away from the someru-ya. "You can trust me, always and absolutely. And I'll be honored to carry on your work."

ensei, I need to continue my ninja training in the valley," Blue Fingers told Dark Fire when he was back in camp the next morning. "I can't explain. But I hope you will trust me and let me go."

"Before, Blue Fingers, you were one of us only because you lived in this camp. But you have proved yourself, and our way is in your heart. Wherever you go, you will always be a ninja."

Blue Fingers smiled. "I *know* I'm a ninja."

"Then you may go. However, your ki double must stay to train under Wooden Fist. Is he all the family you have?"

"My mother also lived through the fire."

Dark Fire's eyebrows rose in surprise. Then he gazed off, thinking. "I must seem very old to you, Blue Fingers. But I am not too old to learn new things. After talking with Falcon about the pain he feels from losing his mother . . . We have little to share, mostly nettle clothing and caves. But if everyone involved is trustworthy, then the mother of two ninja might find a place in our world." He gave a resolute nod. "A clan of five families can become a clan of six."

Blue Fingers spent the rest of the morning learning from Spider how to whistle like a hototogisu bird. After this, anytime he started up the mountain, he would be ushered into camp by a flock of birds.

"I'll be back soon, Taro. Goodbye, Spider," he shouted as he started across the training grounds.

"No goodbyes," Spider called back with a smile behind his sneer. "We'll eat from the same pot again before I've missed you, that much is certain!"

Then Blue Fingers made his way down the mountain.

He hid his shinobi shozoku near where Spider always hid his. The outfit was safer there than at the dye shop, where, if it was found, it would incriminate the man who Blue Fingers sensed was the ninja clan's jonin.

Blue Fingers pushed open the gate of the someru-ya. Standing on a veranda, he saw Mama visiting his foster family . . . so many of those he held in his heart.

He glanced over his shoulder to look up into the hills. Never before had he noticed that from here at the master dye maker's, the view of the mountain was fine. It hit him that this was how it would be from now on: When he was at the foot of the mountain, he would always be looking up at the peak. And when he was up there, he would look down.

Noticing a nearby dye pot, he dipped in all ten fingers. Perhaps he would take a little dye back to camp with him next time he went. Two blue handprints would look splendid between the spider and falcon that branded the wall of the ninja arsenal.

Then he was walking forward . . . no, running now. Because they were calling him. They all held their arms out, and they were all full of smiles.

Author's Note

Although Blue Fingers is a fictional character, his story is based on fact. Ninja clans were crucial during Japan's Warring States period (1467–1568), and sometimes did kidnap village children and force them to join their bands. Ki bearers and ninja names are my creation, but many aspects of the ninja's lives come directly from ninja history. Ninja were ruled by the four directives of the warrior-mystic and did call themselves grass.

They even dislodged their babies' and children's joints so that, as adults, they would be able to dislocate their bones at will. This bizarre ability allowed them to escape from tight bonds, hide in strangely shaped spots, squeeze through narrow openings, and even cast shadows shaped unlike humans. Any ninja lucky enough to live a long life was likely to suffer from terrible arthritis, as Dark Fire does.

It's also true that both males and females were ninja. And as ninja, they shared more equality than they did in the general society of feudal Japan. Female ninja were called *kunoichi*. Besides using long hairpins as weapons, they specialized in close combat and were experts at psychological warfare.

I set *Blue Fingers* in 1545, two years after firearms first arrived in Japan, when they were beginning to appear in outposts away from Edo (now Tokyo). Three Portuguese missionaries brought the first two muskets into Japan. They were passengers on a Chinese junk blown onto Japanese soil by a storm. Their odd faces and mannerisms interested the Japanese—but their guns fascinated them far more.

The local daimyo, Lord Tokitada, bought both guns. After initial difficulties, his swordsmith managed to make copies. Lord Tokitada traded these to other daimyo, and within ten years the new weapons were being manufactured all over Japan. Of course, battles previously fought with swords, daggers, and spears began to look more like gunfights.

Daimyo like Lord Udo fought constantly for their fiefdoms but did so following an honor system called the Code of Bushido. Its rules prevented them from using subterfuge, trickery, or surprise. Samurai sometimes hired ninja to do those stealthy deeds that were essential to waging war but that they could not do themselves without breaking the Code of Bushido.

No other nationality has ever valued swords as highly as the Japanese, and boys from the samurai class were trained from childhood to use them. Still, when guns first appeared, many samurai sought them eagerly. But just as the samurai called ninja dishonorable for using trickery, they soon began to distrust firearms. After all, this new weapon meant they could now be killed by ignorant peasants who had not been trained in the samurai art of swordplay and who didn't even follow the Code of Bushido.

In 1587, Hideyoshi Toyotomi, regent of Japan, used a trick worthy of the ninja to start ridding his country of firearms. He announced that he was going to build such a huge statue of Amida Buddha that he required many tons of iron for the bolts and nails. Hideyoshi forced everyone except high-ranking samurai to donate their swords, daggers, and especially guns to the project. Actually, the collection of weapons was Hideyoshi's foremost purpose for the project. When the "sword hunt" was finished, he had the weapons' metal melted down into a statue of himself.

Hideyoshi's trick worked. He rid the country of most guns, and all but the samurai class of virtually any weapons. After this point, ninja weapons were even more likely than before to be fashioned out of farming implements. After all, farm tools were the only blades to which anyone but a samurai had access. The samurai continued to dislike guns, and from Hideyoshi's day until the late nineteenth century there were very few guns in Japan.

In 1603, the shogun Tokugawa Ieyasu unified the fragmented Japan that is the setting of *Blue Fingers*. He received three hundred ninja like Blue Fingers into his own army. But at the same time, he outlawed ninjutsu practiced outside his army. This drove the ninja into even greater secrecy than before and intensified the sense of mystery already attached to them.

Around that time, Japanese books began depicting ninjutsu as a secret art, and ninja as men and women of mystery and magic. Eventually, the ninja became mythologized in the same way that, over time, a real-life chieftain from the Dark Ages in Britain has become enlarged into the superhuman King Arthur. The modern media completed the transformation of real-life ninja into superheroes. In reality, ninja were former farmers turned spies who battled brutal warlords in the only way they could.

Glossary

Amida Buddha—the embodiment of compassion, wisdom, and enlightenment

bo—wooden pole used as a ninja weapon

chunin—middle-ranking ninja

daimyo—feudal warlord

Edo—Old name for the city of Tokyo

Ganbaro!—We'll stand firm and never give up!

genin—ninja field agent

geta—high wooden-soled sandals with a Y-shaped thong

gokuraku—Buddhist heaven

hakama—a samurai's loose, starched leg covering, worn either split like pants or unsplit like a skirt

haori—short jacket worn over kimono

hototogisu—cuckoo-like bird

Jizo—deity of peace and divine protector of children, often depicted in statues and icons

jonin—top-ranking ninja

kaginawa—rope or chain weapon with a grappling hook

kami—spirit of a certain object, place, or family, which imparts a sense of power, mystery, or strangeness

kami shimo—formal clothing worn by samurai warriors

karma—Buddhist law of cause and effect

ki—energy

kiai—ninja fighting shout, uttered to harmonize oneself with the universe

kimono—long, loose robe

komuso—Zen monks of old Japan

kuji-kuri—finger-moving exercise for the purpose of channeling one's energy *kunoichi*—female ninja

mamukigama—cord and chain weapon

miso—soybean paste

moon—the time between full moons, roughly equal to a month

mudo—stillness training

ninja—outcast warrior trained in espionage, martial arts, and guerrilla warfare

ninjutsu—the art of stealth, as practiced by ninja

nunchaku—ninja weapon made of two rods connected by a short chain

obaasan—grandmother, old woman

obi—wide kimono sash that wraps around the waist several times and ends in a decorative bow at the center back

rappa—another name for a ninja

sakaki—sacred evergreen tree

-sama—extremely polite address when added to a name

samurai—member of the Japanese warrior class, equivalent to the knightly class in medieval Europe. The samurai system contained a hierarchy of lower- and higher-ranking samurai.

-san—polite address when added to a name

sensei—teacher or master

sha—character for healing

shinobi—another name for ninja

shinobi gatana—ninja sword

shinobi shozoku—ninja agent's outfit, worn on missions

shogun—supreme military ruler in feudal Japan

shoji—paper screen serving as a wall or sliding door

shuriken—bladed steel disk, of various shapes, used by ninja as a weapon

someru-ya—dye shop

tabi—padded socks with the big toe separated from the other toes to accommodate the thong of a geta

tatami—floor mat made of tightly bound rice straw

tengu—winged mountain demons with long noses and sharp fingernails and toenails

tenshu—castle tower or keep

torii—gateway often built at the approach to a shrine

tsunami—very large wave caused by an underwater earthquake or volcanic eruption

yumi and *ya*—ninja bow and arrow

zanshin—alertness

zukin—narrow length of fabric used as ninja's hood

For Further Reading

Fiction

Haugaard, Erik Christian. *The Revenge of the Forty-Seven Samurai*. Boston: Houghton Mifflin, 1995.

Hoobler, Dorothy, and Thomas Hoobler. *The Demon in the Teahouse*. New York: Philomel Books, 2001.

———. *The Ghost in the Tokaido Inn*. New York: Philomel Books, 1999.

Kimmel, Eric A. *Sword of the Samurai: Adventure Stories from Japan*. New York: Harcourt, 1999.

Paterson, Katherine. *The Master Puppeteer*. New York: Thomas Crowell, 1975.

Nonfiction

Blumberg, Rhoda. *Commodore Perry in the Land of the Shogun*. New York: Lothrop, Lee & Shepard, 1985.

Chaline, Eric. *Ninjutsu*. Broomall, Pa.: Mason Crest Publishers, 2003.

Craven, Jerry. *Ninja*. Vero Beach, Fla.: The Rourke Corporation, 1994.

Hall, Eleanor J. *Life Among the Samurai*. San Diego, Calif.: Lucent Books, 1999.

Hayes, Stephen K. *The Mystic Arts of the Ninja*. Chicago,: Contemporary Books, Inc., 1985.

———. *Ninja Realms of Power*. Chicago: Contemporary Books, Inc., 1985.

Macdonald, Fiona. *A Samurai Castle*. New York: P. Bendick Books, 1995.

Schomp, Virginia. *Japan in the Days of the Samurai*. Tarrytown, N.Y.: Benchmark Books, 2002.

Following are a few of the books I consulted to research this story. Although none are specifically intended for children, those marked with an asterisk may be appropriate for more advanced readers.

Adams, Andrew. *Ninja: The Invisible Assassins.* Santa Clarita, Calif.: Ohara Publications, 1970.

Bokushi, Suzuki. *Snow Country Tales: Life in the Other Japan.* Translated by Jeffrey Hunter with Rose Lesser. New York and Tokyo: John Weatherhill, 1986.

Campbell, Sid. *Exotic Weapons of the Ninja.* Boulder, Colo: Paladin Press, 1994.

*Cook, Harry. *Samurai: The Story of a Warrior Tradition.* New York: Sterling Publishing, 1998.

*Draeger, Donn F. *Ninjutsu: The Art of Invisibility.* Rutland, Vt., and Tokyo, Japan: Charles E. Tuttle, 1989.

Dunn, Charles J. *Everyday Life in Traditional Japan.* Rutland, Vt., and Tokyo, Japan: Charles E. Tuttle, 1972.

Frederic, Louis. *Daily Life in Japan at the Time of the Samurai, 1185–1603.* Translated by Eileen M. Lowe. New York: Praeger Publishers, 1972.

*Hatsumi, Masaaki. *Essence of Ninjutsu: The Nine Traditions.* Chicago: Contemporary Books, 1988.

———. *Ninjutsu: History and Tradition.* Hollywood, Calif.: Unique Publications, 1981.

Kim, Ashida. *Ninja Mind Control.* Boulder, Colo.: Paladin Press, 1985.

Nitobe, Inazo. *Bushido: The Warrior's Code.* Santa Clarita, Calif.: Ohara Publications, 1969.

Perrin, Noel. *Giving Up the Gun: Japan's Reversion to the Sword, 1543–1879.* Boston: David R. Godine, 1995.

*Sensei, Jay. *Tiger Scrolls of the Koga Ninja.* London: Paul H. Crompton, 1984.

Turnbull, Stephen. *Ninja: The True Story of Japan's Secret Warrior Cult.* Poole, Dorset, England: Firebird Books, 1991.